T

A novel by Patricia Livingston

Cover by Carol Joannette

Northern New York was breathtaking in the fall. The leaves of the various species of trees turned the rolling foothills of the Adirondacks into a patchwork of red, yellow, and orange while the evergreens created a dark contrast. People travelled from New York City and all around the northeast just to take pictures of the natural beauty of this landscape that the locals mostly took for granted. Such a lovely, peaceful world... or so they thought.

Lori wiped her hands on a faded kitchen towel as she looked out the window over the sink. She was an attractive woman. In her mid-thirties, she had smooth, light skin with a hint of freckles on her nose and cheeks, a slender build, and green eyes that tipped up at the outer edges - green eyes that seemed haunted, sad, and secretive.

Beyond their back yard and bare garden, was a woods, adorned in their lovely autumn hues. As cheerful as these colors were, she knew what was coming - winter, and the long, dark months of cold and blinding snow. And the incredible loneliness and isolation from the outside world.

How she hated the winters these days. Her bones ached and she was never warm. The roads were treacherous, and she feared having to drive on them. It felt like the longest season of the year in northern New York. Snow sometimes fell as early as October and continued through April or even May. Lori was hopeful that this year, she would finally be far from here before the coming winter struck the north country.

When she was a girl, she loved that time of year; to go out, all bundled up in a dark blue snow suit, a hand me down from her older brother, Jerry, building forts or going sledding. Sometimes, when Jerry felt magnanimous, he would take her out on the snowmobile, to follow the cow trails through the woods to a frozen pond where they would ice skate together. He took his hockey stick and pucks with him and would slap them at her but she was quick and usually was able to dodge his shots - but not always. The bruises didn't bother her much. They blended in with the ones their father gave her when he was in one of his foul moods. It was the price she paid to spend time with her big brother.

Their mother was a gentle soul. Half Canadian, she was the kindest person Lori had ever known. Her mother tried to shoo her kids out of the house and out of reach of their father's backhand. Mother would try to convince them that their father was really a good man; he just got a little angry since he came back from Vietnam. But Lori remembered him before he went to war, when he tried to teach her to swim at the flat rocks in the Oswegatchie River and nearly drowned her in his frustration with what he took to be her slow learning. She knew he had been angry before he ever deployed, but didn't think on it much. Why bother? Aren't all men angry? she wondered.

Their father had chosen the US Air Force as his career when he was eighteen so he could get off his father's farm and see the big, wide world. A few years later, he came home on leave, met their seventeen year old mother, who was easily wooed with dreams of living in exotic lands, far from dairy country. They married as soon as she turned eighteen and off they went together to not-so-exotic Biloxi, Mississippi where they resided for the next few years.

Two kids later, their father received orders to go to war. As a carpenter in the air force, he was sent with the Army Corps of Engineers to South Vietnam to build bridges and revetments. In later years, whenever company came over to visit, he pulled out the slide projector and screen, and regaled them with tales of his heroism. He sounded like a great man when he told his stories - he was always the smartest or strongest, always knew how to fix others' screw-ups.

Father had picked up his carpentry tools after the war when his enlistment was up, and worked odd handyman jobs around the county. Their mother worked at a small discount store in town and her paycheck was just enough to buy groceries. The kids made due with no name jeans and homemade polyester or cotton shirts. Fabric was cheap in those days - 99 cents a yard, even less on clearance. They didn't really care. They went to school with a lot of kids with as little as they had, or less. Cost of living was relatively low in this county compared to other parts of the state and nearly half the kids they knew were on Welfare. There weren't many kids with nice things in their with the ones their father gave her when he was in one of his foul moods. It was the price she paid to spend time with her big brother.

Their mother was a gentle soul. Half Canadian, she was the kindest person Lori had ever known. Her mother tried to shoo her kids out of the house and out of reach of their father's backhand. Mother would try to convince them that their father was really a good man; he just got a little angry since he came back from Vietnam. But Lori remembered him before he went to war, when he tried to teach her to swim at the flat rocks in the Oswegatchie River and nearly drowned her in his frustration with what he took to be her slow learning. She knew he had been angry before he ever deployed, but didn't think on it much. Why bother? Aren't all men angry? she wondered.

Their father had chosen the US Air Force as his career when he was eighteen so he could get off his father's farm and see the big, wide world. A few years later, he came home on leave, met their seventeen year old mother, who was easily wooed with dreams of living in exotic lands, far from dairy country. They married as soon as she turned eighteen and off they went together to not-so-exotic Biloxi, Mississippi where they resided for the next few years.

Two kids later, their father received orders to go to war. As a carpenter in the air force, he was sent with the Army Corps of Engineers to South Vietnam to build bridges and revetments. In later years, whenever company came over to visit, he pulled out the slide projector and screen, and regaled them with tales of his heroism. He sounded like a great man when he told his stories - he was always the smartest or strongest, always knew how to fix others' screw-ups.

Father had picked up his carpentry tools after the war when his enlistment was up, and worked odd handyman jobs around the county. Their mother worked at a small discount store in town and her paycheck was just enough to buy groceries. The kids made due with no name jeans and homemade polyester or cotton shirts. Fabric was cheap in those days - 99 cents a yard, even less on clearance. They didn't really care. They went to school with a lot of kids with as little as they had, or less. Cost of living was relatively low in this county compared to other parts of the state and nearly half the kids they knew were on Welfare. There weren't many kids with nice things in their school. People with money around here had learned to hide that fact so they wouldn't be asked for a loan from their less-fortunate relatives or friends.

In high school, during her junior year, Lori met with the guidance counselor to discuss her future. She was a bright student, doing exceptionally well in math and science. Mr. Phillips asked her what she wanted to do after graduation - be a teacher, a hair-dresser, or a housewife. Those were the usual choices given to girls in the late 1970's. Lori, growing up with tales of her father's escapades in the air force replied that she would like to join the military and be a fighter pilot. After a brief, stunned moment, Mr. Phillips sputtered, "Lori, you can't be a fighter pilot. You're a woman. Women can't go into combat. Now be reasonable. How would you like to be a nurse?"

In disbelief and stewing over the unfairness of it all the whole bus ride home, Lori ran down the driveway, into their house and pulled out the phone book. She found the number to the local air force recruiter's office and dialed the number on the phone hanging on the wall in the kitchen. She stretched the phone cord as far as she could and closed the cellar door behind her as she stood on the top steps that led into the damp chamber below.

The recruiter she spoke with reaffirmed her guidance counselor's words when he briskly told her they weren't interested in her. They had all the women they needed and really only wanted to recruit more men. As she tried to argue her worth, the line clicked and then she only heard a dial tone.

She opened the cellar door to find her father standing before her, glaring. He wasn't much taller than she; his hair was salt and pepper but he was still beefy and strong. She hoped she might have made him proud of her attempt to follow in his footsteps and serve their country. Instead, he growled at her, "There are only two kinds of women who join the military, and my daughter is neither of them. I will kill you before I let you sign up! Now give up your foolish notion!" Lori saw his hands clenched in fists and knowing what this signaled, she stepped back out of reach.

Her father turned and stomped to his bedroom where he often spent hours, and sometimes days, under the covers in the dark. On those days, their mother would say he wasn't feeling well and kept them as quiet as possible.

Angry, Lori turned and ran out the back door, letting the screen door slam shut and not caring that it would enrage her father. She ran past the shed, through a clearing and entered a wooded area with a small creek running through it. Gingerly stepping from stone to stone, she crossed the creek and ran off into the woods. Near a clearing, an old manure spreader sat abandoned between a pair of dead elms. She jumped in and sat down, hidden by the old, rotten wooden sides.

The manure had been washed away by the weather years ago. Lori had no qualms about lying back against the floor and staring up at the canopy of branches overhead. She could make out the clouds above the bare limbs of the elms. She wished she could join them as they floated across the sky. She wondered where they would end up. Would they would turn into rain and drop to the ground or would they would just dissipate? Wherever they went, it had to be better than here, she thought.

She was just about to let herself cry when she felt a tiny little body skitter across her legs. Holding herself completely still, she waited until a little furry face stared into her eyes. A chipmunk. She had been bringing apples out here and cut them into tiny pieces for him. She felt sorry she had forgotten to bring him something but this time she had come out in a rush. His little paws scratched at her shirt and almost made her giggle. She gritted her teeth and tried to remain motionless so as not to frighten him. He crawled about her torso, and then entered her front pants pocket where he came out with a wrapped piece of Bazooka Joe bubble gum. Tucking it in the pouch of his left cheek, he scampered off into the underbrush.

Folding the kitchen towel in half, the thirty-something Lori hung it over the faucet to dry. She wondered if her husband, Barry would come home tonight. She often asked herself why she married him, but she always came up with the same answer - to escape her father. He was two years older than she but had been held back a couple of times in school so that he was in her graduating class. He was powerfully built, tall with wavy brown hair and hazel eyes. And he was a dreamer, going to make it big one day - strike it rich and live in a big log house in the Adirondack mountains. It sounded lovely and believable - and an hour or so away from her father. So when he asked her to marry him on their second date, Lori said she would think about it. She went home that night and lay on her bed, smiling, looking at the ceiling and dreaming of a life of freedom, where she could be the lady of her own house. A week later, she said yes. He took her to the woods to celebrate where, even though she said no, he took her virginity.

Afterwards, she convinced herself they were practically married, it was ok for them to have sex. She didn't particularly like it but at least it was over quickly. She hoped that once they were wed and lay on a bed, they could take their time. It would be better and she would actually enjoy it. She had heard some of the girls talking in the bathroom at school about how wonderful it made them feel. Lori looked forward to the day when she could feel the same way with Barry.

Not wanting to continue having an intimate relationship outside of marriage, she asked to be taken to the courthouse and wed quickly. It was one of the few times Barry agreed with her, and probably the last. Lori soon found out she was now married to someone worse than her father.

Ten months after their wedding day, Lori gave birth to a son. He was named Barry, Jr. Lori had wanted to name him Alexander and had hopes of a great future for him, but her husband over-ruled her, as usual.

His birth had been hard on her. The baby was too big for her tiny frame and in the third trimester, it hadn't been able to turn inside her. The rural doctor wasn't experienced enough to properly handle the emergency C-section that was required. When it was over, Lori learned she would not be able to have any more children. Barry was indifferent to the news. He had his son, that was all that mattered to him. But Lori had visions of having a number of children who sat with her as she read stories to them. She wanted them to grow up dreaming big and escaping this dreary world, and perhaps, taking her with them. She yearned for daughters she could share secrets with and laugh and teach them what type of boys to date and more importantly, what type not to. She was heart-broken and terribly disappointed, but she kept her grief to herself. She didn't want to hear Barry make fun of her for it, or worse, if she seemed the least bit discontent.

it. She went home that night and lay on her bed, smiling, looking at the ceiling and dreaming of a life of freedom, where she could be the lady of her own house. A week later, she said yes. He took her to the woods to celebrate where, even though she said no, he took her virginity.

Afterwards, she convinced herself they were practically married, it was ok for them to have sex. She didn't particularly like it but at least it was over quickly. She hoped that once they were wed and lay on a bed, they could take their time. It would be better and she would actually enjoy it. She had heard some of the girls talking in the bathroom at school about how wonderful it made them feel. Lori looked forward to the day when she could feel the same way with Barry.

Not wanting to continue having an intimate relationship outside of marriage, she asked to be taken to the courthouse and wed quickly. It was one of the few times Barry agreed with her, and probably the last. Lori soon found out she was now married to someone worse than her father.

Ten months after their wedding day, Lori gave birth to a son. He was named Barry, Jr. Lori had wanted to name him Alexander and had hopes of a great future for him, but her husband over-ruled her, as usual.

His birth had been hard on her. The baby was too big for her tiny frame and in the third trimester, it hadn't been able to turn inside her. The rural doctor wasn't experienced enough to properly handle the emergency C-section that was required. When it was over, Lori learned she would not be able to have any more children. Barry was indifferent to the news. He had his son, that was all that mattered to him. But Lori had visions of having a number of children who sat with her as she read stories to them. She wanted them to grow up dreaming big and escaping this dreary world, and perhaps, taking her with them. She yearned for daughters she could share secrets with and laugh and teach them what type of boys to date and more importantly, what type not to. She was heart-broken and terribly disappointed, but she kept her grief to herself. She didn't want to hear Barry make fun of her for it, or worse, if she seemed the least bit discontent.

He wasn't happy with how things turned out for himself, either. He blamed Lori for holding him back from seeking his great fortune and living his dreams. He even blamed her for the pregnancy coming so soon after they were wed, even though he was the one who had refused to allow her to spend the money to go on birth control.

He took jobs as a hired hand on dairy farms. He was big and strong and able to throw a bale of hay as easily as most men threw a softball. But he inevitably would go on a drinking binge, not show up for work a couple days and get fired. After a spell, Lori heard whispers of what happened while he was out drinking. At first it hurt her feelings to know he was cheating on her, but eventually, it didn't matter anymore.

And her son, her hope and dream for a best friend and protector, was turning into his own father. As a baby, Lori would read to him and carry him everywhere, talking to him, telling him he would be special when he grew up. He would go to college, make lots of money, live in a nice house and they would all be happy together. But then Barry had suddenly become interested in the little tyke the first time he heard him say "Da da." The father latched onto his son, taking him from

Lori every chance he had, and telling him different stories than his mother had - tales of mischief and adventure that await him when he grew up.

When the boy was old enough to hold a tiny pole, around three years of age, Barry took him fishing. When he was just six, Barry took his son hunting, teaching him how to gut their kill. Lori wasn't interested in anything involving blood or death and was glad to not be invited to join them. When her own son started taking swings at her when he was ten years old, Lori's heart and hopes shattered to pieces.

She was twenty-nine years old the first time she saw the door in the woods. That evening, BJ, as they called their son, had taken a swing at her and hadn't missed. Lori had been stunned and held her hand to the stinging red spot on her face. BJ took off to ride his dirt bike to a friend's house, down the long country road between their houses.

Lori had kept Barry's dinner warm until nearly midnight and hoped to talk to him about the boy's violent behavior. Realizing he wasn't coming home, she wrapped his plate in plastic, put it in the fridge and went to bed. She cried herself to sleep. She slept fitfully and near dawn, she awoke to find herself standing in the woods. The sky was still dark but, by moonlight she could just make out a path in front of her. She was dressed in her thin cotton night gown and was surprised that she wasn't the least bit cold.

She looked around, trying to get her bearings, but didn't recognize anything. Nervously, she stood still, wondering what to do, when she heard a little skittering sound in the underbrush. A chipmunk ran out, and seeing her unexpectedly, froze in his tracks. They both stood like this for seconds, maybe a minute, then the chipmunk sniffed in her direction, and perhaps realizing he was not in danger, hopped down the trail, stopping to look back at Lori.

She wondered if he was trying to get her attention, so she followed him. She knew his senses were far greater than her own and if there was a bobcat or bear in the vicinity, the chipmunk would take cover. So she bravely followed him down the path that led deeper into the woods.

After she had walked 100 feet or so, she came to a fork in the path. The one to the left was wide and appeared to be the most travelled route. She would have gone that way but the chipmunk ran toward her then to the right 3 or 4 times. Trusting the little furry guy, she decided to follow him down the less-travelled path, off to the right. After a ways, it got narrower and narrower. Lori began to wonder if she made a mistake. Ahead, through a low-lying, misty fog, she found a door standing upright in her way.

Lori's curiosity about the door took over. There was room to walk around it but something told her to go through the door. The doorknob was of old cut crystal, whitened from the exposure to the weather. She took a hold of it and gave a twist and the door opened easily to her.

She peered through the opening and was surprised to see a clearing with a small assortment of carnival rides. The lights were all lit and the music was playing, but there was no one else around. Lori walked between the rides and suddenly a faceless man appeared. She was startled by his strange appearance and stared at him, trying to make out a face where there was only a gray blur. He never spoke a word but with a flourish of his hand, he directed her to the tilt-a-whirl, her childhood favorite ride. She stepped up on the platform and sat in the car, pulling the bar down onto her lap. The silent man took a hold of the control, gave a squeeze to the trigger and pulled the handle back and the platform started to move.

Lori's car went around and around, spinning faster and faster. Normally she would scream on this ride for the pure joy of it, but this time she didn't. It would seem strange, she thought, screaming when there was no one else but a faceless man there. She held in her pure enjoyment and just let her head roll back as she smiled open-mouthed.

When the ride was over, she stepped down, nodded to the faceless man who gallantly bowed, and she turned toward the door. She noticed it was still open and when she stepped through, she came out of her shed and into her back yard. She tip-toed through the dewy grass and into her house, up the stairs, and to her bedroom. She heard her husband's loud drunken snores coming from their bedroom, and she silently slipped under the covers where she fell back to sleep instantly, with only a bit longer before it was time to get up and start her day.

A couple of years went by. Lori occasionally thought about the door but then she brushed it off as a strange fantasy. Lori was prone to having vivid dreams that in the morning were hard for her to tell if they had been real or not. The door, though, had seemed so tangible, the doorknob, so solid and cool to the touch that she was uncertain for months whether it had really happened or not. Often, when she was alone, she would wonder if dreams were real and her life was just a nightmare.

She had become accustomed to using a thick foundation to hide the bruises on her face and arms. And she really didn't mind that Barry wasn't coming home most nights anymore. He showed up for meals and to change out of his smelly barn clothes and shower, but otherwise, he went to town to drink and then he slept who-knew-where. The nights he did stay home with her were quite unpleasant. He was not a good lover and didn't care if she was a willing partner or not. Sometimes he hurt her but at least it was over quickly, she told herself.

But life was good when Barry was at work, their son was at school, and she was home alone. When she finished cleaning the house and doing the laundry, Lori would often walk in the woods. With each visit, she would travel further and further in, trying to locate the trail that led to the door. She thought she might be able to find it again, if she could just locate that path. Then she would laugh at herself for believing it was real.

One day, she took a trip to town for groceries. As she pushed the cart down the aisles, she noticed an elderly couple walking arm in arm as they both held onto their shopping cart. There wasn't a lot of food in the cart, but they looked happy, in love.

Lori smiled and nodded at them as she passed by, and noticed a strange ache in her chest. As she drove home, she felt incredibly sad. She knew she would never have a love like that old couple had. She wondered how this had happened to her. She was a smart girl, and kind; she should have had a good life filled with love and happiness.

She didn't ask god why it turned out like this. She gave up on him years ago when she was a kid. He never answered her prayers and eventually, she realized praying to a god had the same result as mailing her wish list to Santa. Extreme disappointment.

Lori had quit thinking of divorcing her husband years earlier. He was a proud man and had told her many times that if she ever divorced him, he would kill her. But today, she thought briefly of killing Barry. She could poison him somehow. She knew where he hid the flask that he carried to work with him every day. It wouldn't be hard to slip something into it. But then what?

They didn't have a life insurance policy on him. They didn't even have a savings account. The house they lived in belonged to the farm where he was employed. If he died, old man Snyder might let her live there a week or two but she would have to vacate the premises when he hired his next farm hand. She and her son would be homeless.

Maybe she could get a job. She had no experience and only a high school diploma. In a small town, family connections could be helpful in getting a foot in the door. But in her case, her family name would only hold her back. Most of the Millers were known to be trouble. Besides, Barry didn't want her in the work force. He said she might get some crazy ideas about becoming independent and leaving him. So she kept house, raised their son as best she could, and continued to exist.

This afternoon, she put a hunk of beef and some vegetables in the crockpot, and tucking a couple carrot ends in her pocket, she took off for the woods. She wanted to wallow in her sadness and get it out of her system.

There weren't as many chipmunks in the woods as there had been when she was a girl. She knew her son and his BB gun were responsible for wiping out a number of them in their area.

But a couple of the little critters still recognized her step and came out for a few food scraps from time to time.

She had to go a half mile into the woods to finally see a friendly little furry face. It seemed more nervous than usual and she wondered at that. Squatting down low, she held out a carrot end. He scampered back and forth nervously before he ran up to her, took the offering, tucked it into his cheek, and then skittered back into the underbrush.

Lori found a large boulder mostly buried in the ground, and brushing off some of the loose lichen she sat on its surface, not a foot above the soil. She lay back on it, adjusting her spine to conform to its contour and placed some bits of carrot about her body. A moment later, she felt one set of feet on her, then another, and then another. She smiled as they hopped about her, their little feet tickling her when they touched her bare skin.

When the food was gone and the chipmunks had jumped down, Lori slowly rose up on her elbows to sit upright. She saw their furry little faces peeking out at her from behind some underbrush. She softly asked, "Do any of you know where the door in the woods is?" All but one ran off. He stood still and stared at her and they locked eyes briefly before he disappeared as well.

Arriving home before the bus dropped her son off at the end of the driveway, Lori carried the folded laundry upstairs to put it away. She had finished putting her son's clothes in his chest of drawers and was about to leave his room. It smelled really bad lately. No matter how often she washed his bedding or vacuumed the floor, there was a horrid aroma. She decided to look around to see if he had left food somewhere to rot. Under his bed she found a shoe box she had never noticed before. She pulled it out and lifted the lid, then threw the box away from her. It spilled its contents on the floor - tiny chipmunk and squirrel tails.

No wonder the little creatures were so afraid. BJ probably cut their tails off in the woods after killing them with his BB gun, and left their little carcasses behind as a cruel reminder until the bodies were eaten or carried off by scavengers. She quickly picked up the scattered tails, placed them back in the shoe box and pushed it under the bed.

In a fury, Lori tore through her son's closet until she found what she was looking for - his gun and box of BBs. She took them to the shed and placing the gun on her husband's old anvil, she used his sledge hammer and beat it unmercifully, then wrapped the remains in a rag and buried in the the bottom of the trash bin. The box of BBs she opened and flung into the field beyond their garden.

Back in the house, she stood at the kitchen sink, looking out the window, at the fall leaves, realizing it would be winter before long; she would be snowed in soon and stuck in this house with those two. She wondered if Barry would be home that night, hoping he would stay away. She made herself a cup of herbal tea and sat at the kitchen table waiting for her son to come home from school. She wondered nervously how long it would take for him to notice his weapon was missing. When he came in the house, letting the front door slam behind him, she nearly jumped. Telling herself to relax, she kept a serene smile on her face.

When she heard loud slamming and thuds from upstairs, she knew what he was looking for. After about 5 minutes, he came tromping down the stairs and into the kitchen. It was all she could do to remain calmly seated. BJ growled at her, "Where's my BB gun? Kyle and I are going hunting and I can't find it."

Her back was to her son. Taking a deep breath, Lori turned around and said, I don't know, son. I haven't seen it in weeks. Did you leave it at a friend's house?" She said, trying to sound helpful.

"No, I didn't leave it at a friend's house," he sneered at her. "If I find out you've done something with it, you're going to pay, bitch." With that, he stormed out the door, letting it slam behind him for emphasis.

Lori held herself straight as a board for a moment, before her body started to shake. She knew her son was dangerous, especially now that his body was producing testosterone. She feared going to sleep some nights, wondering if he would come in and murder her in her bed. If he found his bent and broken gun, she didn't know what he would do to her but she knew it would be bad.

Hearing his dirt bike roll to the end of their driveway, she went back to the shed, dug down in the trash bin until she found his beloved BB gun, and pulled it out. She reached for a shovel hanging on a hook on the wall when he stepped into the shed. When she saw him, her hand froze in midair. She could see his dirt bike through a window and realized he must have quietly pushed it back up the driveway to surprise her.

Not knowing what else to do, she quickly grabbed the shovel and held it over her head. Her son was only 15, but the testosterone coursing through his body for the last couple of years had caused a growth spurt. He was big for his age, the size of a grown man.

"I knew you did it, you bitch!" he growled at her.

"Get out of my shed, you little piece of shit, or I'll split your skull" she hissed back.

Lori had never spoken like this to her son before and wasn't sure how he would react. Surprisingly, he smiled and said, "Never knew you had a backbone." Then, more menacingly, "You're buying me another gun. And don't touch my fuckin' stuff again." With that, he turned, and walked out the door. She watched him jump on his dirt bike, start it up and take off down the driveway again.

It took her a moment to hang the shovel back on the hook. Her hands were shaking so badly, she couldn't line the hole in the handle up on it. Once she did, she let it go with a clatter. She held the twisted metal of his gun close to her as she ran out to the woods and pushed it into a hole in a big dead elm tree. Then she sat at its base and put her face in her hands and cried.

When she felt empty of emotion again, Lori stood up, wiped her face with the bottom of her t-shirt and then slowly walked home. She saw her husband's truck in the driveway and her stomach sunk. Rushing inside, she saw he was already seated at the kitchen table, eating the beef stew from the crock pot.

"Where you been?" he asked her.

"Out looking for raspberries for pie," Lori lied. "They aren't quite ripe yet."

'Oh,' was his only response as he continued to push a big hunk of beef into his mouth.

She wasn't hungry but she knew he would expect her to sit with him and eat. So she went to the crock pot and saw there were only vegetables left inside. She didn't really care but she wished just once that he would be a little more considerate. She scooped a couple of spoons into a bowl, pulled a fork from the drawer, and sat in the chair to her husband's right. He told her that was to be her seat so he could swat her easily if she needed it. She tried hard not to need it but sometimes he thought she did anyway.

Tonight, he was quiet. Maybe he was hungover, she thought. Maybe he'll just go to bed and sleep, she hoped.

Lori knew her husband preferred women with curvy figures. So she ate very little to stay slim and keep as straight a figure as she could. Her small t-shirt hung loosely on her thin frame and her jeans seemed to be a size too big. When she had finished, she stood up to carry her bowl to the sink.

"You're too skinny," Barry said to her in a low tone. "Eat!" he barked at her.

"I'm full," she started, but he swiftly backhanded her in the face, stopping any other words from being said. In silence, Lori carried her bowl to the crock pot and took another scoop of stew, then turned to head back to the table.

"More," he ordered. She put the spoon back into the crock pot and pretended to load it again. She did this twice, going through the motions of filling her bowl with food. He seemed satisfied and opened the County Gazette to read the local news and ads. She sat back down and ate in silence, feeling ill with the amount of food she was forcing into her shrunken stomach.

When she thought enough time had passed, she picked up their bowls and went to the sink to clean them. She quietly pushed her uneaten food down the drain so as not to disclose that she had not obeyed her husband's wishes. When she had finished tidying the kitchen, she turned around and was relieved to see her husband had left the table.

She walked into the living room and sat on the couch, curled her legs under her bottom and pulled the afghan off the back of the couch. As she was reaching for her book on the end table, Barry's voice called from upstairs, "Get up here!"

Blanching, she knew what he wanted. A tear trickled down her left cheek as she slowly folded the afghan and put it back on the sofa.

Later that night, as her husband snored, Lori slithered quietly out of bed and tip-toed down the stairs, through the living room and into the kitchen. She slowly opened the backdoor and crept outside. The moon was nearly full and provided enough light for her to find her way across the backyard and garden. At the edge of the garden stood a low stone wall, created by the rocks that Lori picked from the garden each spring and stacked at the edge.

Sitting on the wall of stones, she peered into the woods at the darkness within them. How she wanted to step into that darkness and disappear.

She wondered how she got to this place. She had been a smart girl in school. She could have gone to college. She could have been something. How did she get trapped into this awful existence?

Lori no longer cried these days. What was the point? It only made her face puffy and caused a terrible headache. This, in turn brought on Barry's anger which just worsened the situation. So she learned to just bury her feelings deep in her mind, in a room in her brain that she never visited.

A light breeze picked up and blew her hair and gown. As it travelled past the leaves of the trees, she thought she heard a voice call, "Looooo-reeeee, Looooooooooo-reeeeeeeee."

Sitting bolt upright on the stone wall, Lori listened intently. Was the wind calling her name? Or someone in the woods? Or, was that Barry, awake and looking for her? Full of dread, her heart thudding in her chest, she stood up and ran back to the house, her calloused bare feet not feeling the stones under them.

When she got close to the house, she saw that the door was closed and Barry was nowhere to be seen. She went inside and quickly tiptoed back up the stairs. When she reached the top, she heard her husband's snores still coming from their bedroom.

Relieved, she sat on the landing with her feet on the first step. She doubled over and resting her face on her knees, she wrapped her arms around her shins. She thought briefly of standing up and throwing herself down the stairs. But her fear of surviving with a broken neck and complete paralysis was all that stopped her.

After a while, she went back to bed, slipping under the covers as gently as possible so as not to awake the monster on the other side of the mattress. Her heart was still racing but in her exhaustion, Lori drifted off to sleep.

The next thing she knew, Lori was standing in the woods, a door in front of her. Confused, she looked around to try to get her bearings. How did I get here, she wondered briefly. She recognized this door from years before. It was ancient, carved wood. The crystal knob, still white. She reached for the knob and turned it. Pushing the door open, she was surprised to see not a carnival, but a street, with people walking by, arm-in-arm.

Sitting on the wall of stones, she peered into the woods at the darkness within them. How she wanted to step into that darkness and disappear.

She wondered how she got to this place. She had been a smart girl in school. She could have gone to college. She could have been something. How did she get trapped into this awful existence?

Lori no longer cried these days. What was the point? It only made her face puffy and caused a terrible headache. This, in turn brought on Barry's anger which just worsened the situation. So she learned to just bury her feelings deep in her mind, in a room in her brain that she never visited.

A light breeze picked up and blew her hair and gown. As it travelled past the leaves of the trees, she thought she heard a voice call, "Looooo-reeeee, Loooooooooooo-reeeeeeeee."

Sitting bolt upright on the stone wall, Lori listened intently. Was the wind calling her name? Or someone in the woods? Or, was that Barry, awake and looking for her? Full of dread, her heart thudding in her chest, she stood up and ran back to the house, her calloused bare feet not feeling the stones under them.

When she got close to the house, she saw that the door was closed and Barry was nowhere to be seen. She went inside and quickly tiptoed back up the stairs. When she reached the top, she heard her husband's snores still coming from their bedroom.

Relieved, she sat on the landing with her feet on the first step. She doubled over and resting her face on her knees, she wrapped her arms around her shins. She thought briefly of standing up and throwing herself down the stairs. But her fear of surviving with a broken neck and complete paralysis was all that stopped her.

After a while, she went back to bed, slipping under the covers as gently as possible so as not to awake the monster on the other side of the mattress. Her heart was still racing but in her exhaustion, Lori drifted off to sleep.

The next thing she knew, Lori was standing in the woods, a door in front of her. Confused, she looked around to try to get her bearings. How did I get here, she wondered briefly. She recognized this door from years before. It was ancient, carved wood. The crystal knob, still white. She reached for the knob and turned it. Pushing the door open, she was surprised to see not a carnival, but a street, with people walking by, arm-in-arm.

There were street performers, musicians, jugglers, and magicians. Even mimes dressed in black and white, wandering amongst the couples who passed.

As Lori stood there, a figure appeared before her and gave a low, flourished bow. When he stood upright, he was faceless. She recognized him from the carnival a few years earlier so when he put his left arm out, she was not afraid. Wrapping her right arm into the crook at his left elbow, then placing her left hand over her right hand, they slowly strolled down the street with the others.

Lori smiled at the performers. She had never experienced anything like this before. She had never had a glimpse of the outside world other than in the books she read. Beaming, she turned to look at the faceless man. She thought she saw the sides of his face move as if his cheeks had risen in a smile. She gave his arm a squeeze as if to say thank you.

Wordlessly, he led her to a black wrought iron bench where they sat together to admire a large fountain made of stone carved with images of deer and birds, branches and leaves. As she studied its natural features, it felt familiar to Lori, like her own woods at home. She laughed and pointed when she saw a little chipmunk face peeking from beneath some leaves.

She felt the faceless man's arm slip around her back, his left hand resting on her left hip. He felt warm and strong, sitting beside her, and for the first time in her life, Lori felt safe. Relaxing, she laid her head on his shoulder and smiled when he gave her a firm squeeze.

They sat quietly like this until a sound from behind became louder and louder. Her head spun around and Lori saw a large truck, out of control, barreling toward them. Jumping up, the man took her hand and they ran a few steps, just in time to avoid being crushed.

Realizing they were standing near the open door, Lori reluctantly loosened her hand from the faceless man. Her face looked sad as she gave him a nod. He bowed deeply and before he stood upright, she had slipped back through the door and pulled it closed behind her.

The sky was no longer black, but rather a dark blue. Lori knew it would be dawn soon and her husband would be getting up to go to work shortly. Lifting the bottom of her nightgown nearly to her hips, her long legs unencumbered, she ran instinctively through the woods swiftly until she came out near her garden. She skittered as lightly and quietly as she could up the stairs and quickly slipped back under the covers. Closing her eyes in an attempt to fall asleep for a few minutes, the alarm went off.

Her husband's large hand smacked her on the backside. She turned off the alarm and tried to slip out of bed but he held her down by her hip. Sliding her night gown up to her neck and he, still naked from the night before, Barry climbed on top of her. He didn't believe in foreplay. His reasoning was that if he didn't need it, why should she? Besides, he had to get to work and only had a couple of minutes. That was all it took him to slip it in, give it a few strokes to satisfy himself, and plop down on top of her briefly until his penis shrunk and fell out. Then he got up.

Lori ran into the bathroom to clean up as he dressed. She ran down the stairs and into the kitchen to quickly cook him some eggs and toast and warm up some ham. She placed his breakfast on the table and drank her coffee as he ate in silence. When he was done, he stood up and left without a word.

After she got BJ off to school, Lori went back upstairs and drew a hot bath. She wanted to soak her body to get every bit of

Barry off of and out of her. As she sat in the tub with the water to her neck, she thought how easy it would be to just slip under the surface and drown herself. She had read that drowning was a painless way to die. I could do that. It would be easy. As she imagined it, she wondered what would happen next. Her son would eventually come home from school and look for her to make him a snack. He would search the house, calling out, "Mom," until he found her in the tub, naked!

Then the coroner would take her body into town for an autopsy and he would see the redness down below where Barry had hurt her, his bite marks on her neck and breasts, and the coroner would know what they had done - what she had been subjected to. This was a small town and people would talk. No, she was too mortified to drown herself. At least not today, not in the condition her body was currently in.

Lori was relieved when night fell and Barry had not come home. After BJ had gone to bed, she went out to the back porch and sat on an old wooden rocker, wrapped in the afghan from the couch. She looked toward the woods and thought about the door there. She wondered where it came from and how to find it.

She let her thoughts drift to the faceless man who lived on the other side of the door. He was so gallant, such a gentleman. His manners were so much finer than those of the people she knew in the county. She had read in her romance novels that you could tell a person's birth status by their manners. She wondered if he was an earl, or maybe even a duke. She wouldn't allow herself to be so presumptuous as to think he could be a prince. No, she was no fairy tale princess, worthy of a prince's attentions. She decided she would think of him as an earl. That's it! I'll call him Earl, she thought to herself.

Slowly rocking, her eyes unfocussed on the woods, she heard, "Loooo-reeeeee, Loooooooooo-reeeeeeeeee." Standing up, she stared at the tree-line, holding her breath, she wondered if he would step out from the darkness into the moonlight toward her. When her lungs began to scream for oxygen, she allowed herself to breathe again. When she realized that she couldn't wish him to appear, she knew she had to go to him.

She began walking toward the woods, her mind racing. Where is the door? I don't know how to find it. She stopped halfway through her garden when she heard a loud crack from ahead. Listening, she heard another crack! Someone was coming. Was it Earl? As she stared at the woods, hoping he would appear, some underbrush moved to the side and out sauntered a big black bear!

Lori stood frozen in fear for a moment. She knew that bears had bad eyesight and relied mostly on smell. Keeping her eyes on the black mass, she backed up slowly so as not to stir the air around her. He didn't seem to notice her but was more interested in the not-quite-ripe raspberries on the bushes next to the garden. He grunted as his paw ran through the bushes, pulling the berry laden branches to his mouth. As she stepped backwards, Lori felt the ground change from soil to grass. She spun around and ran through her backyard, up the steps, over the porch and into her kitchen. Pushing the door shut behind her, she locked it and leaned against it, panting heavily. Once her breathing was more steady, she turned around, and peering out the window in the door, she could barely make out the black movement on the other side of the garden.

Relieved, she left the kitchen and headed up the stairs. She told herself it was too dangerous to go outside again that night and ordered herself not to leave the house. Still, she was

She let her thoughts drift to the faceless man who lived on the other side of the door. He was so gallant, such a gentleman. His manners were so much finer than those of the people she knew in the county. She had read in her romance novels that you could tell a person's birth status by their manners. She wondered if he was an earl, or maybe even a duke. She wouldn't allow herself to be so presumptuous as to think he could be a prince. No, she was no fairy tale princess, worthy of a prince's attentions. She decided she would think of him as an earl. That's it! I'll call him Earl, she thought to herself.

Slowly rocking, her eyes unfocussed on the woods, she heard, "Loooo-reeeeee, Loooooooooo-reeeeeeeeee." Standing up, she stared at the tree-line, holding her breath, she wondered if he would step out from the darkness into the moonlight toward her. When her lungs began to scream for oxygen, she allowed herself to breathe again. When she realized that she couldn't wish him to appear, she knew she had to go to him.

She began walking toward the woods, her mind racing. Where is the door? I don't know how to find it. She stopped halfway through her garden when she heard a loud crack from ahead. Listening, she heard another crack! Someone was coming. Was it Earl? As she stared at the woods, hoping he would appear, some underbrush moved to the side and out sauntered a big black bear!

Lori stood frozen in fear for a moment. She knew that bears had bad eyesight and relied mostly on smell. Keeping her eyes on the black mass, she backed up slowly so as not to stir the air around her. He didn't seem to notice her but was more interested in the not-quite-ripe raspberries on the bushes next to the garden. He grunted as his paw ran through the bushes, pulling the berry laden branches to his mouth. As she stepped backwards, Lori felt the ground change from soil to grass. She spun around and ran through her backyard, up the steps, over the porch and into her kitchen. Pushing the door shut behind her, she locked it and leaned against it, panting heavily. Once her breathing was more steady, she turned around, and peering out the window in the door, she could barely make out the black movement on the other side of the garden.

Relieved, she left the kitchen and headed up the stairs. She told herself it was too dangerous to go outside again that night and ordered herself not to leave the house. Still, she was disappointed to awaken in the morning without having gone into the woods.

The following evening at dinner, Lori hesitantly told Barry about the bear. She had to be careful, so as not to disclose the existence of the door, so she said she had seen him that morning, just around dawn, when she had headed to the raspberry patch to see if they were ripe yet. She said she had hoped to pick a few for dessert that night but had nearly come face to face with the bear.

Barry and BJ both jumped up immediately, pushed back from the table, ran out the back door, leapt from the porch without touching the steps, and raced past the garden to where the berry bushes stood. Finding fresh bear prints on the ground, they excitedly talked about baiting and killing the beast. Lori felt guilty for exposing the poor creature to these two monsters, but she so badly wanted to go into the woods and she didn't dare, knowing a bear lived close by.

That Thursday evening, Barry used a drill to make two holes a couple feet apart, side by side in the shed wall facing the woods. Then he used a saber saw and cut the holes larger so that they were each about a foot wide and about two feet high. On the outside of the shed, he screwed a piece of plywood with hinges over these openings, covering them completely. The hinges were below the openings so that he would just need to give it a push and it would fall open.

Barry had Lori save all their food scraps in a coffee can that week. He had tossed scraps in the area where Lori has seen the bear previously for a few nights in a row and confirmed the mess was gone by morning. Friday evening, near dusk, he scattered more food scraps and included some meat fat for an extra-enticing aroma on the ground near the berry bushes. Then he and BJ stayed in the shed, lights out, with the new window open, waiting. Baiting bears was illegal in New York state. Not that Barry cared about the law; he just didn't want to get caught by the game warden. So he and his son were going to kill it with crossbows and arrows. They wouldn't make the noise that his rifle would, possibly alerting someone in the vicinity to call the law on them.

It didn't take long for the black bear to make its appearance that evening. Barry picked up a crossbow and silently handed it to BJ and picked up the second for himself. They already had them cocked and loaded. Barry made some gestures carefully so as not to fire his weapon, but BJ already knew the plan. While the bear had his head down eating, Barry and BJ both quietly lifted their cross bows to the openings and when Barry gave an slight nod, they each took a shot at the bear.

Lori was in the house, in the living room reading a book, trying to take her mind off of what was going on outside. When she heard a horrible ruckus coming from out back, she ran through the kitchen and stood on the back porch. Looking out past the garden, she saw the bear, with two arrows sticking out of its back, standing upright on its hind legs, crying in pain. Barry and BJ each had a hunting knife and were trying to get close enough to stab the bear in the gut. The bear swiped at them every time they came close.

Barry, in his arrogance, thinking that he was impervious to bear claws, not to mention really wanting to own a real bear-skin rug, went in for the kill. Holding his hunting knife low in his right hand, he came in with all his weight and started to lift his right arm to bring the knife into the bear's belly - just as the bear stepped back and brought his left paw forward, swiping it across Barry's face.

Barry's scream rang out like a fire siren. It startled the bear, who stepped back a few feet, spun around and dropped down on all fours, then ran off into the woods, arrows flapping against his back.

BJ attempted to run after the bear but he knew it was hopeless once it entered the safety of the woods. He turned back and ran to his father who was on his knees with his hands to his bleeding face.

Lori stood there a moment, watching the scene unfold. She was glad to see the bear escape and was surprisingly calm about her husband's injury and the apparent pain he was in. She went back into the kitchen, and smiling, pulled some kitchen towels out of a drawer and saturated them. When she stepped back outside, her facial expression was blank as she calmly carried the wet towels out to where the menfolk were squawking. She used one to wipe the blood away from her husband's face. When she did she saw three red lines reappear on Barry's right cheek. It wasn't a deep injury and since the skin wasn't flapping, Lori knew it wouldn't need stitches. She hid her disappointment that his injury was not fatal, and she folded another towel and placed it on his wound and pressed hard. She handed BJ a towel to clean himself up with and handed Barry another to do the same.

After a couple of minutes, she pulled the folded towel away. The bleeding had slowed to just a seep. She put the folded towel back on his face and lifted Barry's right hand up to hold it himself while she gathered the other towels, then took his left arm and led him inside, BJ following closely behind.

She quietly led him to a chair at the dining table, left the room briefly and came back with some iodine, gauze, tape, and ointment. He winced when she cleaned the cuts with iodine on some gauze, but relaxed when she had finished taping more gauze covered in ointment to his face.

When, she had finished, Lori didn't really expect a thank you, but still she hoped for it. Barry growled at her. "Why are you just standing there? Get me a drink!"

Lori ran to the kitchen cabinet, pulled down a small glass but Barry shouted, "Tall one!" so she put it back on the shelf and grabbed a big water glass. She grabbed the bottle of whiskey from the cabinet below the sink and poured about 12 ounces into the glass.

Barry snatched the drink from her hand and, his hands shaking, took a big swig. When he had downed half its contents, he slammed the glass down on the table and said to his wife in a low menacing tone, "You bitch! This is all your fault!" as he pointed to his face. "If you hadn't whined about a bear in your berries, this would never have happened. You better hope to hell this doesn't scar, or God help you, I'll kill you!" With that he picked up his drink, finished it off and held the empty glass out to Lori for a refill.

At the cabinet, as she refilled the glass, Lori wished she had some pills to mix in with the alcohol. At this moment, she didn't care if she killed him or not, or whether she got caught. Life in prison might not be so bad. And being raped by women was probably not as painful as the things her husband did to her.

She went back to the table and handed Barry a full glass and set the half empty bottle of whiskey on the table in front of him. "Can I get you anything else?" she whispered gently.

"What did you say? Speak up, you cunt!" he shouted back.

"I said, can I get you anything else, Barry?" Lori asked her voice quavering.

"No, just get out of my sight. You make me sick," he said, his words starting to slur.

Lori was only too happy to exit the room. She turned and quickly left, and once she was sure he couldn't hear her, she ran, across the living room and up the stairs, down the hall to their bedroom, and without closing the door, she threw herself on their bed face down.

How she wished she could cry. She thought it might relieve some of the pain in her chest. There was such pressure there, like an overfilled water balloon that was about to burst. The pressure seemed to seep into her brain until she thought she heard the whistle of a tea kettle filling her ears.

She kept her head down, hidden by her arms until she heard her son's voice from the doorway. Looking up when he called out, "Mom," he continued, "I hope you're happy. You almost killed both of us, you cunt!" Then he disappeared down the hall and slammed his bedroom door.

Lori was stunned. Her own son called her a cunt. How did she end up with such a vile creature for a son? she wondered.

Then she thought about his words - you almost killed both of us. They echoed in her ears and brain. Lori smiled as she thought about these words. Why have I never thought of that before? she wondered. How would I do it? I could drug them both and then while they were passed out I could pour the gas for the dirt bike on everything, then set the house on fire. She imagined standing at the edge of the woods watching her entire house being consumed by flames, her men with it, then a faceless man reaching out of the darkness and pulling her into his arms and carrying her off to safety.

Yes, what a lovely thought, she told herself. Let me think it through. I wouldn't need this house anymore if I went off with Earl, she told herself. I wouldn't care what anyone else thought of me in the county; I would be far, far away, and I'd never come back to this hell-hole. She surprised herself using this harsh word. Her mother had raised her to be a lady and not to use foul language, but Lori decided not to chide herself for it. Hell-hole, yes, that's what this county is; at least for people like me. Why deny it anymore?

Where would I get the drugs? she wondered. She knew there were places where you could buy illegal drugs in the village, mostly at the bars, she heard. But she had never stepped foot in a bar in her entire life. Her father had put such scare into her with threats of beatings if he ever heard that she had been to one, that it had carried into her adult life. Maybe I could get a prescription for valium, she thought. Her mother had taken valium for years for her nervousness. That's what I would do. I would need to ask her what she said to her doctor to get the prescription.

As she lay there, it dawned on her what she was thinking - planning to kill her husband and son. No, I can't do that! she thought. What was I thinking? That's monstrous! And I don't know how to find Earl anyway. I'd have nowhere to go.

Downstairs, Barry was passed out sitting at the dining table, his arms splayed out as if he was taking a dive into a swimming pool.

Upstairs, Lori fell asleep on top of the covers, fully dressed. She awoke in the woods at the old, wooden door. Shrieking with delight, she reached for the crystal handle, gave it a turn and a push and then quickly stepped through the door opening.

When she came out the other side, she found herself looking at waves crashing on a white sand beach. Her hands flew up to her mouth and she let out a gasp. She had never seen the ocean before but had read about it in some of her novels and seen it on TV. It rumbled and roared as it beat against the sandy shore, the vibrations felt in the soles of her feet. Amazed at the power that the water held, she stood transfixed, staring out at the distance.

As she wondered if a pirate ship would appear on the horizon, she felt a hand on her right shoulder. It pulled on her gently, spinning her about so that she found the faceless man standing before her. As he bowed at the waist, he reached down and with both hands, he lifted her right hand to his face and kissed her tips of her fingers. The softness of it sent a shiver through her body and Lori's knees nearly buckled.

Seeing her unsteadiness, Earl's hands quickly reached out and held her on either side of her ribcage under her arms. Lori, blushing, looked up and realized that Earl had a mouth! His lips were full but firm. She already knew firsthand how they felt on her fingers. She blushed when she wondered what they would feel like on her lips.

"Are you alright, my dearest one?" he asked. These were the first words she heard him say! His voice was deep but soft, like a lion's purr. It made the hair on the back of her neck stand up, and her hand went up to press it down.

Smiling, shining, Lori said, "Yes, kind sir. I am now."

"Please, my little dove, call me Earl," he pleaded.

Gasping, Lori said, "I knew it! I guessed your name was Earl!"

"You know me so well, already, Loooo-reeee. It is as if the stars proclaimed that we must be together."

That sound, her name on his lips, like the wind in the trees! Lori continued to look at his face. She so badly wanted to look him in the eyes but finding none there, she stared at his mouth. She watched his lips part, his strong white teeth and tongue moving between them as he said, "Come, let us walk along the beach, little one." When Lori smiled and nodded her agreement, he spun her about, and placing his right hand on her right hip, his arm across her lower back, he led her closer to the shore. She had arrived barefoot, and, surprised at how the sand and water tickled her feet, she giggled and lifted each foot to try to stop that sensation.

Earl laughed at this and bending at the knee, he slid his arm down below her bottom, then straightened up, with Lori sitting on his right arm as if she was perched on the branch of a tree, his left arm wrapped around her lower legs, holding her steady. He held her tight, keeping her safe as he walked into the water until the waves just touched the tips of her toes. This gentle sensation sent chills up her legs and a rush of blood to the place where they met.

Lori stopped laughing when she felt this and took in a deep breath and held it for a second or two. Earl, felt her body shudder and realizing what she was experiencing, lowered her into the water and turned her so that she faced him. Her head was level with his as he still held her in his arms. She tipped her head back, her lips parting, signaling an invitation to join them to which his responded yes. He brought his lips down on hers and kissed her softly, sensuously, sending shivers throughout her body. Lori had never in her life felt this way and she marveled at the rush, like the ocean's waves were pounding at her chest.

When their lips parted, Earl's mouth went to her right ear and whispered, "You are so sweet, like a virgin. I will be patient, I promise." She felt goosebumps rise on her neck and down her back.

With that, he lifted her in his arms again and carried her out of the water, to the shoreline. Setting her down gently, he placed both hands over her ears and gave a shrill whistle and then removed his hands from either side of her head. Lori heard a thudding sound coming from ahead and then saw a huge white stallion come at full gallop from behind a dune, right towards where they stood. It stopped immediately in front of them and Earl's hands went up to rub his neck.

"This is Belenus. He's my friend. Please, here, touch his neck," Earl coaxed.

Lori had been around many animals in dairy country - mainly cows, some goats, chickens, and ducks, but very few horses. His size frightened her a little but watching how still he stood with Earl's hand on his neck, Lori reached up, and rubbed his neck too. Earl reached in his shirt pocket and pulled out a carrot and then took Lori's hand in his. He held her hand out and flattened her palm, then laid the carrot on it. "Now keep your fingers perfectly straight so they don't get in the way," he said gently, as if talking to a child.

Belenus' head turned toward her hand. He seemed to sense her nervousness and it made him a little jittery as well. His ears twitched as he cautiously stretched his lips out, the soft fuzz of his muzzle brushed against her hand as he grasped the carrot. When he had it in his mouth, Lori laughed and put her hands together, rubbing the place where his muzzle had tickled her. Earl laughed with her and held both of her hands in his.

"Will you ride with me, fair lady?" Earl asked.

Lori had never ridden a horse in her life. She considered it a brief moment, and feeling safe with Earl, she silently nodded her ascent.

Earl took ahold of Belenus' mane and with a jump and a tug he was up on the stallion's back. "Take hold of my arms," he said as he bent down and placed his hands under her arms. He lifted her as easily as a kitten and placed her in front of him. His arms encircled her and he held onto Belenus' mane for steadiness. He clicked his tongue and the stallion began to walk, gracefully along the shore.

Lori sat upright and pressed her back into Earl's chest. It felt solid and muscular - safe. Her legs were draped together on the left side of the horse's chest and she could feel Earl steer the giant beast when he gently pressed his knee into Belenus' ribs.

As they rode silently together, Lori noticed black clouds forming at the horizon. The wind picked up and the clouds began to tumble and roll in their direction. Lightning flickered in the sky and then a low rumble. Belenus whinnied and stopped his forward motion, his front feet stomping in a strange dance.

"It's going to storm. I need to get you back before it gets dangerous," said Earl.

Lori was reluctant to go, but, not wanting to impose on his kindness, nodded. Earl turned the stallion around and his grip around Lori tightened as he gave a kick with both feet. Belenus was only too glad to run in the direction away from the lightning, and so off he galloped. Lori felt his muscles bulge with effort under her legs and she curled them together tightly, back towards Earl's to keep them from bouncing. She instinctively leaned forward and wrapped her arms on either side of the stallion's neck for balance, her face was nearly buried in his mane.

The door appeared before them quickly and the horse's feet slid a little in the sand as he stopped when Earl pulled back on his mane and said, "Whoa, big fellow."

Earl lowered Lori to the ground, then slid off behind her. "Thank you for the exhilarating ride, Belenus," Lori said, as she lovingly rubbed his neck. The gentle giant looked back at her and brushed her face with his muzzle.

"Goodbye, little dove," said Earl. "I hope you return to me soon." With this, he placed one hand under her chin, and tipping her head back, he gave her a soft kiss on her lips. He held the door for her with his left hand, his right hand held hers as he directed her to the doorway. He lifted her hand to his lips for one last kiss on the fingertips before the door closed behind her with a click of the latch.

Lori lay on her bed, half awake, half asleep; her right hand between her legs touching the area that was swollen and tingling. She thought she heard thunder rumbling downstairs, then realized she was hearing metal clanging in the kitchen, she sat bolt upright. Her heart thudded in her chest and, jumping off her bed, she ran down the stairs and into the kitchen to find Barry throwing and kicking her pots and pans around the room. When he saw her in the doorway, he picked up a large stock pot and threw it at her. He caught her by surprise so she didn't have time to duck. The pot hit her on the side of the face and the area next to her left eye trickled blood.

"Why isn't my breakfast ready, you lazy bitch?" he roared.

Lori, dazed, closed her eyes briefly, wishing she could go back through the door. She would much rather face a storm unsheltered than her husband when he was hungover. Opening them again, she kept her eyes lowered as she mumbled an apology. She ran to the cabinet and grabbed a glass, then to the fridge where she pulled out a pitcher of orange juice and poured him a glass. She handed it to him with shaky hands. "Here, honey, have some juice while I make your breakfast. What would you like?"

He ripped the glass from her hand, grabbing her fingers in the action and crushing them. Lori winced but clenched her teeth to keep from crying out in pain. "Food!" he shouted, as sat at the table and opened the County Gazette. Lori put her right hand under her left arm and held it there to try to ease the throbbing pain. With her left hand, she picked up the pots and pans and set them on the countertop. She quickly made him 4 fried eggs, over medium, 4 slices of toast, and fried some leftover ham. She carried a laden plate along with a cup of coffee to him and quietly set them down in front of him.

"Here you are, honey," she said as cheerfully as she could, her voice shaking.

"It's about damned time!" he muttered as he dipped a piece of toast in the egg yolk and pushed it in his mouth. He looked at her standing there and snarled, "Go clean up, your face is a mess."

Lori ran off to the bathroom and closed the door behind her. Looking in the mirror, she didn't recognize herself. The left side of her face was beginning to swell, a bruise had formed, large and purple, and the blood that had trickled from the cut had dried in a crooked red streak down her cheek. She stood motionless staring at the woman who looked back at her with blank eyes. 'Who is that poor woman?' she wondered. 'She really ought to get some help.'

Lori turned on the cold water, bent over the sink and cupping her hands together, washed the blood from her cheek. She continued to hold hands full of cold water to her face, trying to reduce the swelling. It helped the pain in her crushed hand, too. Their well was dug deep in the ground and the water coming from the tap felt like ice; the faucet fogging up from the chill. When her face felt a little better, she reached for the hand towel and patted it dry. Looking in the mirror again, she was startled to realize the woman looking back at her was herself.

'How did that happen?' she wondered. 'I must have been clumsy.'

When she returned to the kitchen, Barry was nowhere to be seen, unlike his dirty dishes still on the table. Lori was only too happy to be alone. She picked them up and carried them to the sink which she filled with warm, sudsy water. She liked to wash dishes. It felt therapeutic. She rubbed them absentmindedly with a wet cloth as she looked out at the woods. Earl was out there, somewhere. 'If only I knew how to find the door during the day,' she thought wistfully. She realized she had made it safely to the door last night and wondered if Barry and BJ had scared the bear off for good.

After cleaning up the kitchen, Lori quickly showered and dressed, then headed to the nearby village. She hadn't been to the library since graduating high school. When she stepped inside, she stopped and inhaled deeply; the smell of old books conjuring up memories of afternoons spent here after school with her classmates. She was not the only teenager who was in no hurry to get home to an abusive parent. The corners of her mouth lifted and she nearly smiled. She looked around at the shelves of books and wondered why she was there. She was startled when she noticed the librarian, Mrs. Thompson had gray hair and glasses! Why, she looked like an old woman. How did that happen? she wondered, her brow furrowed. After a few moments of confusion and panic, she remembered that she, herself was no longer a teenager, but rather an adult with a half-grown son. Relieved with this recollection, she closed her eyes to slow her breathing. And then she recalled why she had come here.

Her heart still racing, she quickly strode over to the reference section of the library, found the old set of encyclopedias, and pulled out the book labelled "B". Setting it on a nearby table and absently sitting down, she opened the volume to search for the word "Belenus." She had never heard of it before and wondered if it was a real word or if she had made it up in a dream. Not knowing exactly how it was spelled, she scanned the pages until she found it. Belenus was an ancient Celtic Sun God - the deity of light, health, and healing.

Celtic! How fascinating. Why would Earl name his horse after a Celtic god? Lori wondered. Her eyes glazed over as she pondered this question. He must be very well educated to know such words, she thought.

She pretended to be reading as she let her mind return to the night before. Earl had a mouth, and he spoke her name, pronouncing it Loooo-reeee. She loved that sound flowing through his luscious, newly-discovered lips. He had an unusual accent. Having never left the county, she hadn't heard anyone else sound as he did. The French Canadians that shopped in the stores in the states had a nasally accent. But his sound was more fluid, relaxed. She realized that his voice reminded her of Ricardo Montalban from "Fantasy Island." His mouth too, reminded her of this actor's. Where was Earl from? she wondered. And why does he live beyond a door in our woods?

"Lori, is that you?"

Startled, Lori jumped. A second or two passed before her eyes fully focussed on the face above her. She stood up and, finally recognizing the woman, she gushed a little too enthusiastically, "Mrs. Thompson!"

"That must have been some very interesting reading, Lori," the older woman said with a kind smile which fell when she noticed the bruises on the younger woman's face. She opened her mouth to say something about it, but decided against it.

"Oh, yes! It's been so long since I've read from an encyclopedia, I had forgotten how enthralling learning could be," Lori said, smoothly. She had had to learn to lie quickly, living with Barry. It came easily to her now. Realizing her manners, she stood up and said, "Mrs. Thompson, I'm so happy to see you again."

"And you, as well, my dear. I remember you spent a lot of time in this library, years ago, always reading, always learning. I expected to see you go off to college after high school." Seeing the hurt look pass across the younger woman's face, gentle Mrs. Thompson quickly continued, "But being a mother is so much more rewarding than any career. Why, you've created life, dear! What a miraculous feat. Something I was never able to accomplish." Her voice drifted away.

Lori smiled and said, "I always felt safe here with you, Mrs. Thompson. Comfortable. So many of us kids did. You were like a second mother to several of us."

A tear formed in the corner of the older woman's left eye and then rolled down her cheek. "That's very kind of you to say, Lori. You've grown into a fine gentlewoman. Your sweet mother must be very proud of you. I'm very pleased to see you are" she hesitated briefly before choosing the next word, "well." She had taken Lori's right hand in hers and gently patted the back of it. This was a gesture she had done so many years earlier, when Lori came to the library to find a book to escape into, a day or two after losing her virginity to Barry. Her eyes had given away her pain and grief, something Mrs. Thompson had become quite good at recognizing in high school girls.

As she had comforted the teenager, she had casually mentioned that there were supplies in the ladies' room she could help herself to. Mrs. Thompson kept a stash of not only feminine hygiene products in the girls' bathroom, but condoms as well that she paid for out of her own meager salary. She never mentioned them, but they were there to be seen in the same cabinet next to the tampons and pads, and she restocked them regularly. How many unwanted pregnancies had this kindhearted woman helped to prevent? If only I had been able to… Lori was ashamed at the thought of regretting her son's existence.

"Mrs. Thompson, I'm glad to see you are well, too. I've missed you. I'd like to come by more often and visit," Lori said, genuinely, smiling.

"Please do, my dear," urged Mrs. Thompson, studying the younger woman's face. "I'd like that very much."

Later that day, Lori quickly cleaned the house. Then she peeled potatoes and carrots and cut them up with some chopped onions and celery, threw them in the roasting pan and placed a fatty piece of beef on top, held it under the faucet for a quick splash of water, then slid the pan into the oven. She almost danced as she gracefully carried a cup of hot tea into the living room, the thick book she borrowed from the library earlier in the day tucked safely under her arm. She set them on an end table and pulled the afghan from the back of the couch, tucked a pillow behind her lower back, and made herself cozy before once again picking up her tea cup and the book.

This was not her usual fare of romance novel or murder mystery. No, this was a tome full of images and tales of the Celtic gods and goddesses. She blushed when she thought about why this subject suddenly interested her, and then, looking out the window, she smiled. Starting at the first page, she began to devour every word, absorb each story, and imagine herself in the drawings of the deities.

She intended to read only an hour or so, but she was so engrossed, she failed to notice the time that had passed until the sound of the smoke alarm in the kitchen broke into her reverie, startling her. She had been relying on BJ's return from school to remind her to turn the oven off, having forgotten he was going to a friend's house after school this afternoon. She jumped to her feet, knocking her tea cup and saucer to the floor, dropped the book on the sofa and ran to the kitchen. Little tendrils of smoke were seeping out the top of the oven and when she opened its door, it billowed out in huge black waves.

She gasped, "Oh, no!" as she snatched the kitchen towel off the counter and grabbed the pot, burning her hands through the fabric. She flung the pot onto the stove top, then rushed to the sink and ran cold water on her hands. Too panic-stricken to cry, she was about to pick up the pot when she heard the front door open and Barry's feet thudding on the floor, nearly as loudly as her heart in her chest.

"What the hell is that God awful smell? Did you burn my fuckin' dinner?" Barry screamed as he strode into the kitchen. When he reached the stove, looked inside the pot, and saw the shriveled black object surrounded by little brown chunks, his face nearly turned purple as he spat, "Fuckin' bitch! You stupid cunt! I worked all fuckin' day and I'm tired and hungry. What the fuck am I supposed to eat? This shit?" With that he grabbed

Lori by the shoulders and dragged her to the stove. Putting his huge hand behind her head he pushed her face until it was almost touching the still hot mess. "Look at it! Do you want to eat that shit? Or maybe you'd rather wear it!"

"Please don't, please, Barry. I'm sorry, I'm sorry," she begged quietly, knowing if she was too loud, it would set him off. He liked her soft and pliant like this.

He held her face close to the pot, the heat still rising and making her sweat. Fortunately, there was no steam to scald her as all of the moisture had cooked away. After minutes or hours of holding her like this, when his arms began to quiver, he released his grip. She straightened up and looking down at her burnt hands, waited. It didn't take long for the back of his hand to sting her cheek, leaving a huge red welt. He stood looking at her for a moment to make sure he left his mark, then, satisfied, turning on his heel, he stormed out the front door without a word. A moment later, she heard the engine of his truck roar, and then gravel hitting the side of the house as the tires spun.

When she was sure he was gone, Lori grabbed a clean kitchen towel and a handful of ice, folded them together, then placed the makeshift ice pack on her swollen cheek. She stayed next to the refrigerator, holding it with one hand for support, cooling her face, her gaze unfocussed. She saw herself reach for the knob to the door in the woods, opening it to see a smiling Earl standing there, then rush through the door and against his firm chest. He wrapped his arms tightly around her and, lifting her feet off the ground, spun her about. How she wished he had been here to defend her. He was so athletic and strong, more lithe, faster than her large, clumsy husband. Barry would be fighting by instinct; Earl would use wisdom and cunning. She felt certain Earl could easily take her husband in a fight. This thought made the ends of her lips curve upwards, ever so slightly.

After cleaning the kitchen and airing out the house, Lori went upstairs. It was late, nearly midnight. She knew Barry wouldn't come home tonight. He thought he was punishing her whenever he slept elsewhere and she was careful not to make him realize otherwise. She drew a nearly scalding hot bath and poured the last of the bath salts her mother bought her this past Christmas into the water. They fizzed and filled the room with a calming lavender scent. Settling in, she closed her eyes and lay there quietly, thinking.

When the water had cooled, and her teeth started to chatter, Lori looked about the room and appeared to be confused. Realizing she was in the bathroom in her house, she pulled the plug, stood up and grabbed a towel, wrapped it around her and walked to her bedroom.

She brushed her shoulder length auburn hair until it dried, bending over to flip her tresses over her head, trying to give it some volume. She didn't own a blow dryer. They never had money for luxuries like that. Nor could she afford to go to a beauty parlor for a haircut, so Lori gave herself a trim whenever she felt it needed it. She had gotten pretty good at it; keeping the edges mostly straight.

She didn't own any real makeup, but she did have a couple of sample lipsticks, eye shadow and mascara that a woman had given her when she stopped by her house, trying to sell her some Avon products. Lori had never worn eye makeup as a teenager. Her father used to say to her, "If you want your eyes blackened, I'll do it for you." She had never learned the art of applying eye shadow or mascara so they were left untouched. Pale pink lipstick, however, was allowed in her childhood home. It was considered lady-like to wear a subdued, natural color.

Lori had eyed the woman's samples and picked up a bright fuchsia lipstick. She pulled the cap off and held it in front of her face, admiring the bold, sassy hue. It was rich and luscious, something she was sure her father would wholly disapprove of and call her a ten cent hussy it he ever caught her wearing. She put it back down and thanked the Avon lady for stopping by and explained that she just never wore make up. The Avon lady thanked her for her time and before she turned and left, handed her a small bag of samples, one of which was the very shade of lipstick she had been admiring.

She had tried the rich reddish-pink lipstick only once, that very night. Lori wanted to see Barry's reaction when he came home from work and hoped he would say something kind to her. He had a reaction alright, but not the one she had hoped for. She had a hard time getting lipstick stains out of the bedsheets the next day. After that, she kept the bag of samples safely hidden away in the back of her top dresser drawer.

Tonight, she dug in her drawer for the bag and pulled out the fuchsia lipstick. She carefully applied it to her lips, then pressed them together and puckered. She looked in the mirror over her dresser and frowned. The rich color emphasized the thinness of her lips. So she applied it a little thicker, going just above and below the natural outline of her mouth, then stood back. Yes, fuller lips looked so much better. And the bright color drew the eye away from the red hand print on her left cheek. It made it almost disappear. Just a few pinches to her right cheek and, there, she just looked like she was blushing a little.

In another drawer, she had hidden away a long black nightgown which she pulled out with a flourish. Dropping the towel to the floor then kicking it aside, she slid the nightie over her head. It was cut low, with spaghetti straps, and was a size too big which, on her thin chest nearly exposed her nipples. Lori had found it in Barry's truck one day and had taken it. If he noticed it missing, he never said a word to her about it. She had never worn it for Barry, but had washed it and put it away.

A thin woman, with messy auburn hair, a swollen red cheek, a clown mouth, and an ill-fitting night gown stared into the mirror. Looking back at her was a beautiful woman with porcelain skin, seductively thick hair, luscious full lips, her lovely breasts pouring out the top of a long black evening gown.

Lori smiled at this vision who smiled back at her with lovely, straight white teeth. The ladies curtsied to one another, and then reaching for each other, they swirled around the room together as both hummed, "Some Day my Prince Will Come." When their waltz was over, Lori was gone and the beautiful woman stood in the middle of the room, studying her image in the mirror. Satisfied with her appearance, she pulled the covers back on the bed and sat down. She reached over to Barry's side of the bed and pulled the string that was attached to the light fixture on the ceiling. The single light bulb went dark and the beautiful woman lay back against Lori's pillow and closed her eyes in eager anticipation.

Sleep came swiftly that night as it threw a dark blanket of comfort over this fragile woman. The first hours, Lori's body went into healing mode, and began repairing the new damage to her face and hands; her mind was at complete rest in total blackness. But in the early morning, before dawn, the beautiful woman found herself wandering about in the woods. The moon was full and sent arrows of light between the tree branches and onto the path, pointing the way. She strode gracefully and with confidence, her head high and her shoulders straight. The night was silent, as if in awe of her beauty. The only sound heard was the occasional skittering sound of tiny feet in the pine needles and the hoot of a barn owl in the distance.

She seemed to know exactly where to find the door and walked straight to it. She reached for the crystal door knob, wrapped her slender fingers around it and twisted, but the door knob would not turn. She tried again, and then, frustrated, commanded, "Open this door!" Silence. "Open this door at once!"

She stood with her ear against the door, holding her breath, and listening for sound from the other side. Nothing. Using both hands, she beat against the ancient wood open-handed, bang, bang, bang! "Earl, it's Lori! Let me in!" she shouted, a hint of anger in her tone. She pressed her ear against the door. Still, it was completely quiet. She grabbed ahold of the door knob with both hands and using her whole body for torque, she groaned as she tried to force it to turn without success, then kicked the door in frustration, and stood waiting, breathing heavily.

After a minute or two, Lori's shoulders slumped and her head dropped forward. The spaghetti straps of her nightgown slid down her arms. She grabbed a hold of them and held them up close to her neck. A sharp pain ripped through her chest, and then the tears started sliding down her cheeks. She dropped to the ground, wrapped her arms around her knees and hid her face behind them. As she sat like this, she thought she heard a creaking groan. Lifting her swollen red face from behind her knees, she saw that the door had opened, just a bit.

Lori gasped and jumped to her feet. She lifted the top of her nightgown to wipe away her tears, thankful that she was not wearing mascara and gave a nervous little laugh. Then she fanned her face with her hands briefly before poking her head around the door and peeking inside.

"Loooo-reeee, my fair lady, you came, just as I had dared to hope," said Earl, with a deep bow.

Lori stepped through the doorway, then threw herself into Earl's arms. "Earl, I didn't think you were here!"

"Oh, my little one, I will always be here for you," he cooed into her ear, holding her close to his chest.

Lori, confused, wondered about this statement. She thought she remembered beating on the door to no answer, but now she wasn't sure if that was real or not. No, Earl was always here for me, he said so himself, she thought. I must have just imagined that he was gone. How silly of me.

"There was someone else here, just moments ago," he continued. "A stranger. But I kept her out. Only you are allowed to come here, Loooo-reeee, my love. No one else may pass through that door."

Lori smiled at this and tipped her head back to look at Earl's face. It wasn't as blurry as it had been on her last visit here. Now he had a nose. It was straight and prominent, and gave him an aristocratic appearance. Her smile widened, and Earl, recognizing this look, leaned in for a soft, gentle kiss. Lori's arms went up and wrapped themselves around Earl's neck, and she pulled his face closer and pressed her lips harder into his, her breaths coming quicker.

Lori felt something swelling, growing hard against her pelvis, but then Earl's hands went to her arms and gently pulled them away. He stepped back and holding her hands, said, "Ah, my sweetness. I feel your passion too. But we must be careful. We shall wait until we are married."

Earl's words took all of the sting out of his actions. Lori looked up at his face, wishing she could look into his eyes, and beamed with radiant happiness. Married! she thought. Married to Earl!

Suddenly, her face fell as she remember. I'm married to Barry. Turning her back to Earl, she fought back the tears. What will I do? she wondered. Barry will never let me have a divorce.

Earl's arms came around her waist and he pressed his chest against her back. His face came over her right shoulder and leaning down, he whispered into her ear, "I know you are not free to marry me, yet. But you will be one day. And I will wait for you, however long it takes, my dove."

Lori spun about in his arms and pressed her face against Earl's chest. Their hearts beat in rapid unison, ba-dum, ba-dum, ba-dum. I will never be happier than I am in this moment, she thought. I never want to go back through that door again.

As if he read her mind, Earl said, "Looo-reee, my pet, I wish you could stay here with me forever. But I know you have responsibilities on the other side of that door. I understand that I cannot keep you here with me now, but must wait until you no longer have those commitments. I will be patient, I promise." With that, he gave her a gentle squeeze and kissed the top of her head, as if he was comforting a child.

Earl tucked her hand in the crook of his arm and walked a leisurely pace though a nearby wrought iron gate. On the other side was a lovely botanical garden filled with flowers of all colors in full bloom. The air held a heavenly scent; butterflies and hummingbirds flitted about and songbirds trilled. Lori gasped at the wonder of it all. Her senses were nearly overloaded with so much beauty and, overcome with emotion, she dropped to her knees and wept.

Earl knelt beside her and wrapped his arms around her shoulders. "I'm sorry, Earl. I don't mean to be such a baby. Please forgive me. I don't want to ruin our time together," Lori pled.

"There is nothing to forgive. I understand you well, my fragile flower," Earl soothed. He helped her from her knees to a sitting position in the grass and they sat with their backs against a tree where they remained for a spell, in silence.

After a time, Earl finally spoke, "My dearest, I hate to say these words, but it's time for you to go." Lori nodded silently. The smile left her face and her eyes lost their glow. "If only you were free, my love. You could stay here with me forever," Earl whispered longingly, his lips against her hair.

He stood, then reached down with both hands and pulled Lori to her feet. Placing his right hand on her lower back, his fingers on her hip, he led her back out the gate and to the door.

"Will there ever come a day when we don't have to say goodbye to one another?" Lori asked sadly. Her hands went to Earl's solid chest, her fingers clutched frantically at his shirt. She tipped her head back for a long soft farewell kiss before reaching behind herself, she turned the knob and stepped out. The door closely behind her gently with a click and then she was instantly whisked away to her bed.

Days passed, and then weeks without returning to the door. Lori brooded silently, wondering if Earl had forsaken her. She heard his words over and over in her head, "If only you were free, my love. You could stay here with me forever," the last word echoing in her mind.

She wondered if she was banished from Earl's world until she could come to him, unencumbered with a husband and a son. I may never be free, Lori thought, panic-stricken.

Depression settled in and clung to her heart like the fog in the woods. Preoccupied with her thoughts, Lori was sometimes clumsy. One particular evening, feeling weak from having not eaten that day, she was about to drain a pot of boiled potatoes into the sink when suddenly the pot became too heavy for her to carry. She dropped it on the floor, boiling hot water and potatoes splashing everywhere.

Barry was sitting at the table reading the paper and drinking his whiskey. BJ sat next to him holding the funny pages. The clammer of the pot startled Barry and he jumped to his feet. Seeing the majority of his dinner ruined, he stomped across the floor and pulled back his fist. Seeing what he was about to do, Lori stood up tall and straight and glared at him. "Don't you dare, you filthy piece of garbage," she hissed at him.

The expression on her face took him aback. She was almost unrecognizable. Barry had never seen his wife look so regal. But hearing her call him such a name threw him into a rage. After a brief pause, his fist came forward into her face, not once or twice, but three times, the third time just grazed her cheek as she was already heading for the floor. BJ was standing next to him urging him on, "Hit her again, Dad!"

Barry shouted at her, "Get up you bitch! Clean up this mess!" Lori lay completely still on the floor in a crumpled heap. "Get up, you lazy cunt!" Barry squatted down and grabbed her by the shoulders and shook her. Lori's mouth hung open and her head bobbled about. He bent down and put his ear to her mouth and listened. He couldn't hear her breathing!

In a panic, fearful that he had killed her, Barry looked around the room frantically. Stopping to think a moment, he scooped his wife up into his arms and carried her out to his truck, BJ right beside him, holding her feet. They placed her in the passenger's seat without buckling her in, then Barry jumped into the driver's seat and BJ hopped into the bed. He started the truck, the engine roared, they drove the the end of the driveway, made a sharp right and headed down the road. About a mile away, just before coming to a sharp bend in the road, Barry stopped the truck, got out and pulled Lori over to the driver's seat while BJ jumped out of the back. Barry walked to the side of the road and found a heavy rock. He placed it on the gas pedal and when the engine as revving at a fast rate, he reached through the open window and pulled the gearshift lever on the steering column to drive and watched his truck take off down the road. When it reached the bend, it went off the road, through a fence, up a tree and then flipped upside down. He and his son stood transfixed for a moment.

Even Barry was shocked by how well his plan turned out. He ran to the truck and crawled through the open window and fumbled around until he found the rock. He pulled it out and threw it in the woods, then the two began the hike back to their house.

When they got home, Barry began to clean the sloppy mess when he thought he heard a siren in the distance. He stopped and went to the front door and opened it. Yes, it sounded like an ambulance. Someone must have driven by and saw his truck and called 911. He quickly returned to the kitchen to finish cleaning and ordered BJ to help. He knew that shortly, the sheriff's office would send someone to his door to tell him his wife was dead.

The men ate the meatloaf that had been holding warm in the oven. Barry washed their plates and forks and put them in the dish drainer. He stared at it a moment, then pulled a third plate out of the cupboard and a third fork from the drawer and ran them under water, and then placed them both in the dish drainer as well.

He stood back and looked around the room. It looked perfectly normal. He sat back down at the table and took a swig of his whiskey. He sent BJ to his room with the order that he was not to speak with anyone about what had happened that night. He knew he could trust his son. They were two of a kind and both of them were rotten.

What was taking so long for the deputy to come to his door? he wondered. Barry's face turned ghost white when he realized he hadn't put Lori's purse in the truck with her. She wouldn't have left the house without it. He leapt to his feet and began to pace as he punched the air for not reminding him to do this. BJ was lucky he was upstairs or it would have been him who had been punished for this oversight.

Barry nearly jumped out of his skin when he heard a loud ringing sound. He ran to the phone hanging on the kitchen wall, then took a few deep breaths to try to relax himself before he picked up the handset and squeaked, "Hello?"

A woman's voice spoke, "Is this Mr. Miller, Lori Miller's husband?"

"Why yes," Barry said smoothly, "this is Barry Miller. What can I do for you?"

"Mr. Miller, I'm calling from Hepburn Hospital. Your wife has been in a serious car accident and is currently undergoing surgery. You should come right away," said the woman, urgently.

Barry's mind when blank. Surgery? They don't operate on dead people. "Surgery?" he gasped. "Is she going to be alright?"

"Mr. Miller, you should come right away," was her curt answer.

Barry's hand shook as he hung the phone back on its cradle. What if she lives? he wondered. What if she tells them what happened? I'll go to jail. He paced the kitchen again and then stopped suddenly and shouted, "Mother fuck! I wrecked my goddam truck for nothin'!"

Barry went upstairs and found Lori's purse still in their bedroom on top of her dresser. He opened it up and dumped the contents on their bed. He stirred the items until he found her keyring and snatched it up. Then he went down the hall to the bathroom and washed his face, combed his hair and gargled with mouthwash. Taking one last look in the mirror, he noticed the frightened look on his face. He gave himself a little shake and then attempted to look sad, worried. He wrung his hands together and looked at the floor, then peeked again at his reflection. When he was satisfied, he gave a nasty chuckle and went out the door.

He had trouble squeezing his large frame and beer belly into Lori's '75 Datsun B210. He hated this tiny car but the price had been right - free - when Lori's grandmother passed away and left it to his wife. He reached under the seat and pulled the lever, sliding the driver's seat as far back as it would go, his knees still nearly touched the steering wheel.

He slowed down as he drove past the "accident scene" on his way to town. Stopping the old beater, he threw it in park and with his headlights shining on the path his truck had taken not long ago, he got out of the car for a better look. He could see the tire tracks running through the weeds and tall grass, the crushed fence and underbrush, and the patch of missing bark on a large maple tree. "I shoulda lit that truck on fire," he grumbled.

Realizing they may be wondering what was taking him so long to get to the hospital, he crawled back into Lori's car, shifted the gear back into drive and floored it. Nelly, as Lori liked to call her car, hesitated a brief moment, not understanding this command, then took off down the road, nearly reaching a whopping 65 miles per hour. It was probably the first time in this tiny car's life it had ever gone faster than 50 and its little engine whined in protest.

When Barry walked into the hospital, he stopped and looked around. He hadn't been in the building since BJ was born. That time, they had gone through the emergency room entrance. Visiting the sick and dying neighbors or family members was always Lori's job so the main entrance was a mystery to him. The volunteer at the information desk saw him looking lost, called to Barry and waved for him to come over. Once he had been told where to find his wife, Barry went to the elevator and took it up to the surgical floor.

He checked in at the desk and then went to the empty waiting area. The only surgeries done this time of day were emergencies and in this rural area, those came pretty infrequently. He had dozed off in an uncomfortable chair when the surgeon came in and called his name. Still slightly buzzed from the whiskey he had before dinner, Barry, eyes still closed, growled, thinking he was being disturbed at home. Then he opened his eyes a slit, realized where he was and who had awoken him, he jumped to his feet, rubbed his eyes and smacked his lips, trying to dispel how dry his mouth felt.

The surgeon caught a whiff of Barry and instantly stepped back. He wanted to pull his mask back over his face but fought off that urge. "Mr. Miller, I'm Doctor DeFranco. Your wife just came out of surgery. She had some internal bleeding in her abdomen which we've stopped. We're going to have to send her downstate for a neurosurgeon to take a look at her. Her head trauma is pretty substantial and we aren't equipped to handle those types of injuries here.

Barry's eyes were wide with fear. What was all of this going to cost? he wondered. Aloud, he asked hesitantly, "What would happen if we kept her here? I hate to send her so far away. She's never left the county before." He thought it sounded believable, as if he cared about Lori's feelings.

Doctor DeFranco responded, "Your wife could die. You can't keep her here. You must let us send her downstate!"

"You can't make me let her go. I want to keep her right here, near me!" Barry said, puffing out his chest and bouncing on his tiptoes like a little bantam rooster.

The surgeon's face clearly showed his disbelief. Was this man that stupid? he wondered. He decided to try a different tack. Speaking slowly and enunciating every syllable, he started, "Mr. Miller. I know you love your wife and think that by keeping her here you are doing what she would want. But I am sure she would want to continue living a normal life. She would want you to let her go to Syracuse to see a neurosurgeon, so she can get better and go home to you."

Barry, realizing he wasn't going to win this argument by bluster decided to bluff instead. "Look, doctor. I love my wife and I want her to come home to me as quickly as possible. Our Lord and Savior, Jesus Christ will heal her. Just get her ready as quickly as possible and then I will take her to our home where God lives and He will make her whole again. We have rights, you know. You can't go against our religion!"

Your only religion is taught by the Reverend Jack Daniels, thought Dr. DeFranco. But what could he do? He couldn't go against his patient's husband's wishes. Not while she was unconscious and unable to make her own medical decisions. "Very well. Once your wife regains consciousness, I will release her to your care." He was buying time, hoping that when Lori came to she would agree to being sent to a larger facility in Syracuse or Rochester where she could receive the expert care she needed in order to fully recover.

Sneering, Barry responded, "Good. I'm glad you finally see things my way."

Dr. DeFranco turned on his heel and left the room without another word. He didn't want to spend any more time with this Neanderthal than was necessary. He felt like he had lost several brain cells just by breathing the putrid air around him and was afraid if he stayed any longer he would punch that jackass in the face. And as a surgeon, he couldn't risk damaging his hands. As he stormed down the corridor, he thought about Lori's facial injuries. The bruises had looked distinctly fist-shaped. In this poor county, domestic violence was common and he had treated many battered women over the years. The marks on Lori's face were too broad to be a steering wheel imprint but resembled injuries from a beating. He had brushed that thought aside before, but now that he had spoken with her husband, his suspicions were back and he became even more determined to help this poor woman.

Ten days passed before Lori came out of the coma. And for all of that time, Barry barely ate and what little sleep he had was haunted by dreams of being locked up in prison. The first few days he had spent evenings at the hospital at her bedside in the hopes that if Lori came to, he could silence her with intimidation before she could tell anyone about what he had done. But when she didn't awaken, he began to feel hopeful that she might die in her sleep.

When the phone rang that tenth evening, Barry had been drifting off in his old, beat up brown recliner with the newspaper in his lap. The paper fell to the floor when he jumped up to answer the call. BJ came running down the stairs, saw him listening to the phone, and watched his father's face whiten as the blood drained from it. He held his arm when he saw him sway on his feet. When Barry placed the handset back on the hook, BJ waited less than a second before saying, "W-well?"

Barry said absently, "She's awake. We can go see her now."

BJ felt the bile rise in his throat. "What are we going to do, Dad?"

"We had better hurry up and get down there before she talks. I've got to shut her up," he said. "Grab your coat and let's go!"

Lori's eyes opened slowly when they walked into the room. They stood next to her bed side by side, both with their hands behind their back as if they were about to be scolded. Lori smiled broadly at them and said, "I'm so happy to see you two. I've missed you both so much."

Stunned, BJ and Barry looked at each other gape-mouthed and then in unison, looked back at Lori. "I hope you boys have been eating well while I've been away. Barry, darling, you looked worn out and thin."

Barry, realizing he should say something, said, "How do you feel, baby?"

"Oh, I'm drowsy but I feel fine," said Lori.

"Good, that's good to hear," said Barry, a little nervously. Then added, "Do you remember what happened?"

"No," said Lori, "but I heard the nurses say I had an accident in your truck. I'm so sorry, sweetheart. You loved that truck. I don't even know why I would have been driving it instead of my car."

Barry had given this a lot of thought in the last several days and said quickly, "You offered to run out and gas it up for me so I wouldn't have to leave early in the morning to drive to the gas station before work." Lori had never done this before but it was the only somewhat plausible excuse he could come up with. It seemed to satisfy her because she just nodded her head.

She had a serene smile on her face as her eyelids dropped and she slept again. BJ turned to Barry and asked, "What's up with Mom? She didn't sound like herself."

Barry's eyes were still on her face, watching her closely for a sign that she might be listening. "I don't know, but I think we might be off the hook," he whispered, just in case she was faking sleep.

"What do we do now?" asked a nervous BJ.

"We watch her," replied Barry in an ominous tone.

Dr. DeFranco walked quickly into the room. "Hello, Mr. Miller," he said and stood waiting a moment for an introduction to his son. When none was given, he nodded to BJ and said curtly, "Young man." Lori had heard his voice and her eyes opened slowly. "Well, hello young lady! I'm Dr. DeFranco" said the doctor in a friendly tone. This surprised Barry since he had never heard him speak this way before. "Gentlemen, if you could please leave the room for a moment, I need to examine my patient."

Barry's chest puffed out like it always did when he felt a fight coming on. Lori spoke gently, "Barry, darling. It's ok. Really."

Barry knew it would look bad if he argued now. He stood still a moment looking back and forth at their faces - Lori smiled encouragingly and the doctor frowned his disapproval - and then he let his chest drop down to his gut again. "Come on, BJ. Let's go get a coffee. We'll be back in a couple minutes," he said to the room, shooting a dirty look at the doctor before he turned and went out the door.

When he had finished his examination, Dr. DeFranco said, "I'd like to send you downstate to be examined by a neurosurgeon."

"Neurosurgeon?" said Lori incredulously. Then, realizing she would be sent far from the door in the woods, and Earl, she quickly said, "I feel fine. I don't think that will be necessary."

Dr. DeFranco's eyes narrowed as he watched her expression, then asked, "Mrs. Miller, do you know how you got your injuries?"

"Yes, doctor. I had an accident driving my husband's truck," was her answer.

"Did you get all of your injuries from the accident?" the doctor asked carefully.

"Why yes, of course. How else would I have gotten hurt?" she responded innocently.

Yes, how else, indeed, he thought to himself. "Mrs. Miller, we ask this of all our patients so please don't take this the wrong way, but do you ever feel afraid at home? Is there anyone there who hurts you in any way?"

"Oh, no, doctor. Our house is full of love and kindness," Lori replied, quite convincingly. The doctor studied her face a moment and then she added, "Are my husband and son back yet? I hope they can come in soon. I am so eager to make sure they are doing ok without me at home to take care of them."

Doctor DeFranco replied, "Yes, they are standing out in the hall. I'll send them in," and with that he left the room as briskly as he had entered earlier.

Lori was released to go home about a week later. Barry and BJ were both amazed and confused by her transformation. She was calm and self-assured. She lavished them with affection and carried herself with confidence. Barry would have appreciated this change in her if it didn't make him feel inferior.

A day after she was settled in their house, Barry decided she needed to be reminded who's boss. Before heading out to work, he told her he expected the entire house to be spotless and dinner ready when he got home, knowing full well she had orders from the doctor to take it easy the next several weeks. When he walked in the front door that evening, he smiled with satisfaction. The mess he and BJ had made while Lori was in the hospital was all straightened up and wonderful smells were coming from the kitchen.

He hung his coat on the hook next to the front door and then turned and noticed Lori sitting stretched out the couch smiling up at him and holding a book in her hands. At that moment, a strange woman came out of the kitchen and wiped her hands on her apron. Lori stood up, and still smiling, introduced them, "Barry, this is Mrs. Smithers, from up the road. Mrs. Smithers, this is my husband, Barry."

"How do you do, Mr. Miller. Dinner is ready whenever you are," said Mrs. Smithers, who turned and walked back into the kitchen.

"Who in the fuck if that?" Barry snarled at Lori.

"That's our maid and cook, Mrs. Smithers. You said you wanted the house clean and dinner ready when you got home. I'm certainly not in any condition to do it, so I hired her to do it for you," said Lori.

"I can't afford to pay her. Fire her!" Barry hissed. With that, he grabbed Lori by the shoulders and was about to shake her.

"Hold on there, bucko," she said, tauntingly. "You don't want to send me back to the hospital, do you? Dr. De Franco's got his eye on you. And he probably wouldn't appreciate it if you undid some of his fancy stitching."

Barry held onto her shoulders and glared into her eyes. Lori fearlessly looked directly back into his, a slight smirk on her face. She could see the wheels turning in his head as he calculated the risk of knocking her around a bit. When he was certain she wasn't bluffing, he let go of her with a huff and said, "Fire that woman, now!"

"Fine," said Lori, "but you and BJ will have to start helping around the house until I am fully recovered. Besides, it's time BJ learned how to cook and clean, anyway."

"No son of mine is going to do woman's work!" With that, Barry folded his arms high over his chest for emphasis.

"Are you going to do it all, then?" Lori sneered.

"No. Not on your life." Barry unfolded his arms and held his fists on either side of him, obviously struggling to keep from punching her in the face.

"Then BJ will clean house and cook dinner after school, instead of stalking the woods everyday looking for some little creature to kill, and you can do the laundry on the weekends," Lori announced.

"And just what are you going to do during all of this?" Barry asked.

"Why, I will supervise and instruct," replied Lori haughtily, her chin held high.

Lori had been given six weeks of recovery time and took advantage of every bit of it. They didn't have insurance on the truck, so Barry had to sell what was left of it for scrap metal and was paid next to nothing. He took Lori's old beater for transportation leaving her stranded at home, for a bit. Four weeks after her surgery, she felt well enough to use BJ's dirt bike to run to town to go to the library. Of course she didn't let the guys know it. They would expect her to go back to her job as their drudge.

When she walked into the library, she looked around a bit, as if lost. Mrs. Thompson saw her confused look and walked over to where Lori stood. "Hi, Lori. I heard about your accident. I'm so sorry. How are you feeling?" She was looking at the bruises, not fully healed on Lori's face, now a pale green and yellow. She had seen bruises like this before on the faces of so many women who came in here for a momentary escape.

Lori glared at the older woman, and then asked, "Do I know you?"

"You've known me since you were a child," said Mrs. Thompson, sounding hurt. "Don't you recognize me? I'm Mrs. Thompson, the librarian!"

"Oh, yes, of course I do. I'm sorry, the medication I'm on makes me a little dopey. Mrs. Thompson, I know you," Lori said with a chuckle.

Mrs. Thompson took the younger woman hands in her own and held them. "It's alright, I understand. I take it that you didn't come to see me, then."

Lori, thought quickly then said, "Something drew me to this place. It - it must have been you."

A wide smile spread on the old librarian's face. She put her arms around Lori and gave her a close hug. She seemed awkward at this show of emotion. She seldom touched the students for fear of sexual harassment charges and she still thought of Lori as a teenager.

Lori stood stiff, adding to the awkwardness of the moment. Mrs. Thomson's arms fell and she stood there a brief moment before turning and walking away quickly, her hands on either side of her face trying to cool them, embarrassed by what she had just done.

Lori wandered around a bit and then finding the books she wanted, she sat at a table and read sections of each. She kept a close eye on the clock on the wall above the door. When it was getting near the time for BJ to get home from school, she put the books back on their shelves, gave Mrs. Thompson a wave, and left.

She put the dirt bike back in the shed and topped off the gas from the can on a shelf. She hadn't used much at all but didn't want to make BJ suspicious, in case he kept track of that sort of thing.

Lori still had a couple of weeks until her recovery period was over. This gave her some time to come up with a plan and make some arrangements to execute it. She smiled at that word, execute. Yes, I have a plan to 'execute" and then laughed, almost maniacally.

A week later, when BJ walked into the house after the school bus had dropped him off at the end of the driveway, Lori called her son to come to the kitchen. She greeted him with a ham and cheese sandwich and a glass of milk. BJ was only too eager to gobble his sandwich and chug the milk. Lori was smiling at him when he was finished and he shot her a suspicious look. She continued to smile at him with as much maternal warmth as she could muster and placed her hand on his shoulder.

"Son, I've been thinking. I have some money I've stashed away that I think we could really use now. I can't get to where it's hidden though, would you help me?" Lori asked.

"What do I get in return?" asked BJ.

" I suppose satisfaction for a job well done isn't enough," said Lori as he shook his head in the negative. "Well then, how does $100 sound?" she asked.

BJ's eye lit up, then the suspicious look returned. "One hundred dollars? Where did you get that kind of money?" he asked.

"I've got much more than that stashed away for a rainy day. I've been skimming from the household budget for years, saving for a hard time like this. The medical bills are coming and we need it now. But I put it in a place that I am too unwell to reach. I'm afraid I'll rip my stitches. That's why I need your help, darling," she said.

He looked at his mother and studied her face intently. She was different since the accident. She was loving and kind, and she didn't back down from him or his father. She wasn't skittish and afraid of them anymore. He didn't like it, not one bit and he didn't trust her. But she was looking at him with an innocent expression appearing so open and honest. He wanted to believe her. One hundred dollars sure was tempting. If the bitch doesn't cough up the money, I'll yank her hair out. That won't show if she runs to her doctor friend to tell on me, he thought.

"Alright, where is it? In the attic?" he asked.

"No, it's outside, in the pasture near the woods," she replied.

"In the pasture? How do you keep money in a pasture?" he asked, his hands on his hips expressing his disbelief.

"I have it in a metal storage box. It's weatherproof. There's cash and some gold coins my grandmother left me in the box," she said excitedly.

He watched her face a moment, waiting for a smile to break, but when he realized she was dead serious, he said, "Ok, I'm in. How do I find this box?"

"I'll walk with you," said his mother. "It isn't far from here." Concentrating on the thought of a $100 pay day, BJ didn't give any thought to his mother being physically able to walk to the pasture near the woods. He was impatient to get there and set a quick pace, Lori, easily able to keep up beside him. When they got to the fence, she pulled up on a strand of barbed wire and stepped on another to widen the gap and let her son squeeze through. Then she followed behind him as they entered the pasture where old man Snyder let cows graze. Stepping on field stones to avoid the landmines the cows left behind, Lori led him to an old abandoned well. The original farm house had stood on this spot a century earlier. The chimney and and a small section of a stone wall were all that was left behind.

Lori pointed at some boards and stones and said, "The box is down that old well, stuck in a crevice on the side. You can climb down the side by holding onto the stones, like rock-climbing. They hold me and you aren't much heavier than I am. They'll hold you too."

BJ looked nervous. She was afraid he would back out so she asked slyly, "You aren't afraid, are you? I went down there every month, when I was well."

BJ puffed his chest out, just like his father. Lori gritted her teeth together, her jaw flexed when she thought of this. How she despised that man. She wasn't about to let her son grow up to be a monster, like his father.

"Naw, I'm not afraid. That's a piece of cake," he bragged.

He moved the stones and then the boards that were over the opening in the ground and looked down a moment. Then he lay on his stomach on the ground and slid backwards, dangling feet first into the hole. Once he got a foothold, he started descending, step by step. "How far down is the box?" he asked just before his head disappeared.

"Oh, only about twenty feet," said Lori, causally.

Only twenty feet? he thought. Only? That's pretty deep. This is worth more than $100. I think I'll just take half the stash off the bitch.

Lori stood over the opening and watched her son climbing lower and lower. "You're almost there, just a couple more steps down, sweetheart" she encouraged.

I can't believe that cunt comes down here every month, BJ was thinking, stewing about the climb. He was getting tired, his hands were in pain with the effort. He noticed it got lighter in the well and he looked up. His mother's head had disappeared. "Mom? Where are you?" he called out, sounding almost like a little boy.

A moment later, her head reappeared, "I'm right here, son. I had to get something." With that, he saw an object falling towards him, then felt it hit his head. A rock! It was the size of a grapefruit and dazed him for a moment. He nearly lost his grip.

BJ yelled out, "Stop it , you stupid bitch! You're gonna get me killed!"

"Yes, my baby boy. Mommy knows. Mommy isn't going to let you grow up to be a monster like your father. Now be a good boy and die!" Another stone fell and hit his right shoulder and made his arm drop to his side. He was dangling by his left hand and scrambled to grab a hold with his right hand again.

"You fuckin' cunt! Wait 'til I get outta here. I'm gonna knock the shit out of you and then I'll tell Dad and he'll take his turn!" Angry and scared, BJ was frantic to escape. Clawing at the rocks trying to grab a hold, he was struck again. His screams began to rise from the opening in the ground, shrill, like a wounded animal. Lori raised a large stone over her head, then flung it downwards with all her might. It struck his head, hard, drawing blood. BJ let go with both hands and put them up to protect his skull. He fell another ten feet and hit the water at the bottom with a splash. He went under for a moment before his head bobbed above the surface. The water was still quite deep in this old well and felt like ice. "Mom! Please!" he whimpered. His screams had turning to grunts as he used all of his energy trying to find something his stiff, frozen fingers could grasp to pull himself up. Rocks continued to beat him until the cold overpowered him and he lost consciousness, and then, stopped breathing.

Trying to control her heavy breathing, Lori waited several minutes, listening. There was no sound coming up from the well. She had read last week at the library that in 50 degree Fahrenheit water, hypothermia could kill in minutes. She had also read the ground water temperature map and knew that where they were in northern New York, the water in the well would be somewhere between 42 and 47 degrees. When she was certain that he would never attempt to crawl out of the well again, she laid the boards back in place and then put stones back over them, careful to lay them on the dark spots of the boards where they had lain before. Looking around, she studied the stone wall and made sure it wasn't noticeable that it was slightly smaller than before. She stood still for a moment, realizing she was no longer a mother and letting that sink in, she smiled as she gazed upon her son's grave. "Goodbye, BJ. I'm sorry I ever brought you into this world. You were such a disappointment to me. And now, somewhere in the world, I've saved a poor girl from a future life of misery. I guess I've just done my good deed for the day."

She turned and flipped her hair back from her face, then tiptoed back across the pasture, stepping only on the field stones on her way, then crawled through the barbed wire fence, careful not to catch her clothes on it before heading back to the house, alone.

She washed and dried BJ's plate and glass and put them away. She checked the clock and saw that almost 2 hours had passed since her son had gotten home. She opened the phone book and dialed the kitchen wall phone. When someone on the other end answered, she said, "Hello. This is Mrs. Miller. Did my son, BJ, I mean Barry Miller Junior stay after school today?"

After a moment, she said in a fearful voice, "He hasn't come home yet. I'm worried. Could you check with the bus driver to see if he dropped him off at our house?" After a pause, she said meekly, "Thank you."

A half hour later, her phone rang and she answered it immediately, and after listening, she answered in a panicked voice, "He did? Well, I haven't seen him. Thank you."

She hung up the phone and smiled. Then she dialed several of BJ's friends' houses, asking if he was there. She was still on the phone when Barry came home. He bellowed, "I don't smell anything cooking. What the hell's going on?"

Lori hung the phone back on the hook and ran to him, her hands on his chest, and cried, "Barry, BJ hasn't come home from school. I called the school and they say the bus driver said he dropped him off at the end of the driveway. I've been calling all of his friends. Nobody's seen him. I'm really worried. He's been so good about coming home and doing his chores."

Barry stood still a moment, not saying a word. Lori laid her head on his chest to hide her smirk as she thought to herself, I can hear the clunking of his brain as the moron tries to figure this out. He brusquely pushed her away as he ran outside. He came back into the house and announced, "His dirt bike is still in the shed. That lazy boy never walks anywhere."

Barry paced the kitchen, then stopped and asked, "Did you hear any cars on the road today?" They lived on a dirt road and nobody could sneak by. Tires would throw up stones and struts and shocks would squeak over the ruts.

"I'm sorry, I was napping. I didn't hear anything," and then began to cry softly into her hands, hiding her lack of tears.

"You called all of his friends?" he asked. When she nodded silently, he said, "Then I'm going to have to call the cops."

She knew it was a difficult decision for him to make. Barry was constantly in trouble and hated calling the sheriff's office, but he loved his son, and so decided to make this sacrifice for him.

Less than an hour later, a deputy was at the front door. He took their report and then went back to his car to use his radio there. Barry used this time to make himself a quick sandwich for dinner. He pulled the ham out of the fridge and said to his wife, "Where did all the ham go?"

Lori lied, "BJ made two sandwiches for his lunch today with it."

"Two?" asked Barry, "does he always take two sandwiches?"

"No," said Lori, then pretending to be startled, she asked, "Do you think that means something? Like he was planning on not coming home right away tonight?"

"Maybe," said Barry hopefully. "Are you sure he didn't say he was going somewhere after school today?"

"He never said anything to me. He didn't say anything to you?" Lori asked, deflecting the fault from herself.

Barry thought a moment. He had been drunk, as usual last night. Did my son say something to me that I forgot? he wondered. He was still racking his brain when he heard the knock on the door. He strode over and opened it quickly. The deputy was standing there and said, "We're putting together a search party. Call your neighbors and friends. Tell 'em to bring flashlights and lanterns. It's going to be dark soon."

They searched all night. Barry had suggested they check the woods and so this was where they concentrated. Several searched along the creek that ran nearby, following it for miles.

Lori stayed inside the house with some of the neighbor ladies, helping to keep coffee going, while others assembled and wrapped sandwiches that volunteers carried out to the searchers. From time to time, Lori would stop to rest with her hands holding her abdomen, putting on a good act that she was still very sore from her surgery.

The following day, the sheriff ordered a wider search area. Lori was stunned that no one had noticed the old well and decided that the searchers didn't want to dodge landmines to physically search the field. Since it was flat and wide open other than the old chimney and stone wall, she thought perhaps they had shone their light upon it from the edge of the woods, and seeing nothing out of place, they ignored it.

The searchers left the area and most of their neighbors went home at dawn to milk their cows. Barry showed up around 3 that afternoon, looking haggard and worried. Lori had been sitting, resting, but when her husband arrived, stood and winced, then trotted to him and asked if they had any luck. Barry, feeling more helpless than mean didn't answer but just shook his head.

Not long after he had come in, there was a knock at the door. Lori answered it, holding her abdomen as if in pain. A man stood on their front stoop in a blue suit and yellow and blue striped tie. He was not quite six feet tall, had dark brown hair, a straight, aristocratic nose, and steel gray eyes. "Mrs. Miller?" he asked. Lori, preoccupied with this man's handsome looks, only nodded, so he continued, "I'm Detective Bill Davis of the sheriff's office. May I come in?"

Lori backed up and held the door open wider, smiling, said, "Yes, of course, please come in, detective."

Barry glowered at the man, then asked, "What do you want?"

Lori, appalled at her husband's lack of manners, said, ""Barry! The detective is here to help us find BJ." then turning to the detective, asked wide-eyed, "Aren't you?"

"Yes, ma'am, I hope so," he replied.

"Please, sit down," said Lori, directing him toward the couch. "Can I get you something to drink? Coffee? Soda?"

"No, ma'am, I'm fine. Are you alright, though?" he asked, noticing her holding herself. He seated himself on the sofa where she had pointed. Lori sat gingerly on the other end while Barry plopped onto his recliner.

"Oh, yes. I'm just recovering from surgery after a car accident a few weeks ago. I'm still a little tender," said Lori, with a shrug.

"Yes, I heard about that. It was a bad accident, a roll over. I am glad to see you are recovering nicely," the detective said.

Lori gushed, "Oh, yes, detective. My son and husband have been so helpful while I've been recuperating. BJ cleans the house and cooks dinner. Barry does the laundry. I can't do much of anything, yet."

The detective had a little notepad in his left hand and scratched something on one of the pages with the pencil he held in his right hand. "What did you just write?" Barry asked suspiciously.

"Just keeping notes. Nothing to be concerned about," said the detective, turning toward Barry.

"I know what you detectives do. You try to blame people. You're going to say one of us did it. Well, I wasn't even here when my son disappeared," said Barry, belligerently.

"That's right, detective. I was sleeping on the couch when BJ's bus dropped him off. Barry wasn't here," said Lori, reassuringly.

"How long had you been sleeping when the bus came?" asked Detective Davis, not looking up from the pad he was writing on.

"I don't know," said Lori, thinking. "I had taken my pain medication around 2 and it knocked me out shortly after, so maybe an hour before the bus came. I woke up around 4:30 and called out to BJ to start his chores. When he didn't answer, I searched the house and shed for him. When I didn't find him, I called the school. They said he got off the bus here. I was worried, so I called his friends."

"So you didn't notice anything out of the ordinary that afternoon? You didn't hear anything?" asked the detective.

"No, nothing. Barry asked me if I had heard any cars on the road but I didn't hear a thing. I'm afraid I was out like a light," said Lori guiltily. "I hope you can help us. He's my only child and I can't have any more." With that, she wept softly.

"Ok, you got what you came for," interrupted Barry. "You can go now."   "I'm not finished yet, Mr. Miller. Do you know anyone who would want to hurt your son?" he asked, watching for a reaction.

"It wasn't me. I loved that boy," said Barry.

Both the detective and Lori caught his use of the past tense. The detective quickly wrote something in his note pad while Lori turned her face away to hide the smile that almost appeared. She couldn't believe her good fortune. Barry just stepped on a landmine and left a big, squishy footprint behind.

"Where were you yesterday afternoon between 3 and 4 pm, Mr. Miller?" asked Detective Davis."

"I, I was at the farm next door, milking cows and shoveling shit," stammered Barry.

"Can anybody corroborate that?"questioned the detective, and when he saw Barry's questioning look, "was anyone else with you who can vouch for your whereabouts?"

"N-no, I was working alone. I'm the only hired hand on the Snyder farm. Old man Snyder leaves me to finish up in the afternoons while he goes inside for a nap," he answered nervously. "Now, you aren't thinking I hurt my boy, are you? 'Cause that's just nuts. I might smack him around a bit when he acts up, but that's all," his words drifted off when he realized he wasn't helping himself.

Lori piped in, "That's right. He only beats him with his belt once in a while, when he needs it. He always stops when the boy has had enough."

"I see," said Detective Davis. "And what sorts of things does he do to need it?"

"Oh, the usual," said Lori, sounding helpful. "Not doing his chores, leaving his dirt bike in the yard, getting into his father's whiskey and condoms." Then she put her hands to her mouth as if she had accidentally said more than she should have.

Barry was staring at her, his mouth agape. His face turned purple with the exertion of holding himself back from choking the life out of her. The detective's pencil was flying away on that notepad. "I thought you couldn't have any more children, Mrs. Miller." The he turned to her husband and asked, "Your condoms, Mr. Miller?"

"Naw, I don't have any of those. Lori's on pain meds. She doesn't know what she's sayin'," Barry said, and tried to laugh it off but it sounded more like a whine.

Detective Davis sat back and watched these two. Mrs. Miller was being open and honest, trying to help, but Mr. Miller was belligerent, holding back information, and acting awfully guilty. He also noticed the looks Barry was shooting at his wife and how she didn't seem to want to look back at him. "Mr. Miller, I have a lot more questions. I need you to come down to the station with me."

Lori kept her head down and forced her mouth into a straight line so as not to smile. Barry angrily jumped to his feet, his hands clenched in frustration and helplessness. Realizing that losing his temper wouldn't help matters, he forced his hands to open, wiggled his fingers, and just nodded his head. He went out the door without a word to his wife as Detective Davis followed immediately behind him.

When the door latch clicked shut behind them and Lori was alone, she smiled, closed her eyes and whispered, "It won't be long now, darling Earl. One down. Just one more to go."

Lori slept alone that night. This time she knew who her husband was with - Detective Bill Davis. She chuckled every time she thought about how scared Barry looked when he left. She wondered why, since obviously he hadn't been involved in BJ's disappearance. She chalked it up to his past bad experience with the law. He had been hauled to jail numerous times on public drunkenness. He had never been arrested for it, just kept overnight in lock up to keep him from causing trouble. Whiskey made him mean and sometimes his smart mouth got him smacked around a bit by the guards at the county jail.

As soon as she had crawled between the sheets, she was fast asleep. She knew right where to go and she was at the door in the woods in no time. She stood there for a moment, and gave herself a little shake. Making her face look sad, she reached for the door knob and gave a twist. It was locked! How does this door know I am not that weak, mousey Lori?

She slapped herself in the face several times, pulled her own hair, and squinted her eyes tight, trying to force tears. When she felt good and battered, she reached for the knob again. Still locked. She stood staring at the door for several moments. Her eyes narrowed as she realized this door was locked to everyone but her old, battered self.

She flew from the door and hovered over her own body before re-entering it. She lay there, in a lucid dream state and realized that in order to help herself, she needed to become a real victim again. She spent the rest of the night planning on how to make this occur.

The next day, in the afternoon, Lori heard the front door slam, then loud stomping across the floor before Barry's voice bellowed out, "Cunt! Where the fuck are you?"

Lori had been sitting at the kitchen table, drinking tea. She knew what she was in for and knew that it had to be done. She sat there quietly as she heard him yell out, "Cunt!" again.

When he came into the room, he saw her sitting quietly at the table, ignoring him. "Why didn't you fuckin' answer when I called you?" he growled.

"Oh, were you calling me? I thought you were crying for your mother," Lori sneered.

She knew the detective would have warned him off beating her. And she knew that his mother was his weak spot. But desperate times… In less than a second he had entered the room, lifted her by her upper arms and threw her against the wall. She landed on the floor in a heap. "Bitch! Leave my sainted mother out of this!" He picked her up by the back of her neck with one hand and held her in the air and shook her as she cried out in fear and pain, before slamming her against the wall again. She whimpered briefly as she slid down to the floor and remained there, rolled herself into a fetal position, and then slipped off into delightful unconsciousness.

Lori arrived at the door almost instantly. It was opened a crack for her so she pushed it further and peeked inside. Earl was waiting for her, with a huge smile that went all the way up to his steel gray eyes.

Lori's heart leapt when she realized Earl had eyes. She was pleased to see that he was quite handsome, and then it dawned on her that he looked a lot like Detective Davis. She threw herself into his arms and held him tight.

"Looo-reee, my sweet! It's been so long. I was afraid you weren't coming back to me," cooed Earl.

"I'm sorry, Earl. I haven't been well. And then I got lost and couldn't find my way back here," she cried.

"Oh, my little one. You don't have to apologize to me. I'm just happy you are here." Earl held her close for a moment before he pushed her away to look at her face. Their eyes locked and she felt drawn deeply into them. She felt such love emanating from his being, surrounding her with warmth and comfort, it overwhelmed her and tears began to slide down her cheeks.

He wiped them away with his thumbs and said, "There, there. Please don't cry. I only want your happiness."

She smiled with wet eyes, and said, "These are tears of happiness, my love."

Earl turned so that they were side by side. His right hand enveloped her left hand and he led her to walk down a path through thick bushes. They turned a bend and the path suddenly widened to reveal a small grassy clearing overlooking an enormous canyon. They walked to the edge and looked down. Far below them raged a river; above them soared eagles. There were jagged rock mountains in the distance, and beyond them, the ocean. It was all so majestic and powerful. Lori stood transfixed at the wonder and the beauty of it all.

Earl stood beside her quietly for a moment before he whispered, "This only begins to show you the strength and magnitude of my love for you."

Lori gasped at this. Then doubt crept in. What did I do to deserve such devotion from a man as perfect as Earl? she wondered. Fearful of the answer, she still had to know. "Earl, why do you love me so?" she asked.

"Looo-reee. You and I are each half of the whole. We are one and the same. Without you, I am nothing. You complete me and I exist only for you," he said vehemently.

Lori listened intently to his poetic words but wasn't satisfied with his response. He didn't answer the question - Why me? What's so special about me? she wondered. She continued to gaze over the natural beauty before her and leaning against his strong torso, decided just knowing he loved her was enough. She didn't need to know why.

An unknown period of time passed as they stood this way - minutes, hours. Lori couldn't tell. The sun began to set over the mountains and splayed out a blanket of rosy red, orange, and pink across the clear blue sky. Lori wondered if Earl had the power to orchestrate such an exhibition. He seemed capable of anything, why not this?

He put his hand against her lower back and guided her to a blanket on the grassy clearing with a large wicker picnic basket sat. Earl held her hands as he helped Lori to ease down onto the blanket. He plopped beside her still holding her hands, then pulled her into his arms. Tipping her head back in invitation, Lori's small frame was drawn against his powerful chest, and he leant down to kiss her. His left arm went up to cradle her neck while his right hand went to the ground for support. He gently lowered her to a lying position as he hovered over her prone body.

He kissed her again, softly, his lips quivering with his restrained passion. Lori's body was molten against the blanket and she was ready for anything he wanted to do to her.

Then he lifted his head and gazed deeply into her eyes. She looked back into his eyes of steel and saw dark gray clouds forming a storm, rolling and whirling, mesmerizing her soul.

Oh, please, make love to me! her mind begged, hoping he would read her thoughts and obey.

"Looo-reee, my love. Are you free yet? Please tell me you are. I want you so much," he breathed against her lips.

She so badly wanted to lie to him, but she knew she never could. It would ruin everything they have. Closing her eyes so she wouldn't see his reaction, she answered, "Almost, my love. I have no son anymore."

Earl exhaled deeply. She felt his disappointment. Opening her eyes, she rushed on, "I'm sorry, I've been unwell. But I am better now, stronger than ever. The next time I return, I promise you, I will be free. Completely."

She held her breath waiting for his response. He slowly smiled at her showing his strong white teeth, so straight and perfect. Then he said, "No son, that is good, my love. You are halfway there. I knew you could do it. You are so much stronger than you think you are, my brave lioness."

Relieved, Lori, smiled widely, allowing herself to revel in happiness. She placed both hands on either side of his face and lifted her head up to his to kiss him again. "Earl, it's you that gives me strength," she whispered.

"Perhaps I only awaken your strength, my flower, but you've had this power within you all along. You're stronger than you think, my love," then, smiling, the dimple in his right cheek popping, he added, "I'm starving. Let's have something to eat and drink." With that, he rolled over and sat upright. He opened the basket and pulled out some fresh strawberries, slices of cheese and meat, and a bottle of champagne.

He popped the cork and poured their glasses. Handing her a glass, he held his in the air and said, "A toast, to being halfway there. May the other half come easily and swiftly."

Relieved with this reaction to her news, Lori lifted her glass and clinked it against his, then put it to her lips and drank it down. It made her tipsy, woozy. She stood up and held her head. "You aren't well, my love. I'm afraid it's time for you to go back, anyway," said a concerned Earl.

"Yes, I think it is. I can't stay here now," she cried. Turning away, she saw the door was immediately in front of her. She wondered briefly how it had moved, but let that thought slip past. "I'll be back, as soon as I possibly can, my love. I'll be a free woman the next time you see me."

"I will be here, anxiously awaiting your return, my sweet," his voice drifted away as she slid though the door and it closed behind her.

Lori awoke on the kitchen floor, still in a fetal position. She sat upright and realized she was dizzy, as she had been after drinking that glass of champagne. The room was completely dark. What time is it? she wondered. She tried to stand but was too unsteady. She crawled the short distance to the kitchen cabinets and opened one of the doors to pull herself to her feet. She leaned on the countertop to steady herself and nearly jumped when she heard a voice from behind her slur, "You're still alive? I can't fuckin' believe it."

Barry! He was sitting at the kitchen table. He had left her on the floor, hoping she would never come to again.

Lori held her head with one hand while still holding herself upright with the other. The throbbing inside her skull was nearly blinding her and a loud ringing in her ears was deafening. She could barely make out what Barry had just said to her but she heard enough to become infuriated. Hiding her pain and anger, Lori pulled from her reserve of energy and stood upright, turned toward Barry and smiled.

Barry was either too drunk or too stupid to see that within her smile was a look of pure hatred and deviousness. He saw what he wanted to see - a weak woman, ready to please her master.

Not particularly wanting another beating right now, she decided to act submissive. "I must have been exhausted," said Lori apologetically. "I don't know why I fell asleep on the floor like that."

"'Cause you're a stupid cunt, that's why," sneered Barry. "Stupid and lazy." His words drifted off at the end and his forehead was touching the tabletop.

Lori had seen her husband drunk hundreds, maybe even thousands of times over the years but he had never been this far gone. He must be taking BJ's disappearance hard, she thought. If I didn't feel so horrible right now, I would taunt him about it. But as bad as he looks, I don't know if I can out-run him in this condition. She stood perfectly still, not wanting to rouse him, and when she heard his loud snores, she tip-toed from the room.

Once in the living room, she headed to her rocking chair, turned it toward the window and then sat on it, looking out into black nothingness. Her mind wandered until her eyes caught her reflection on the glass. She turned her attention to study the woman who was staring at her. She saw a gaunt face, with wide cheekbones above sunken cheeks, and thin, straight lips. Ignoring the bruising and swelling, as well as her small pointed chin and upturned nose, her gaze went next to her eyes. They appeared too large for her small face and while their green color was not discernible in the dark reflection, they somehow appeared to glow. They had captured Lori's thoughts and drew her in. She wondered what was behind those eyes, what secrets they held. She had to find out. She didn't realize she was leaning in toward the glass until she noticed that her image had fogged up from her breath.

Briefly startled, she sat back in her rocker. She looked at the glass and recognized herself in its reflection. She wondered why she hadn't known herself just a moment earlier. Then, the pain in her head reminded her that it was still there. She brushed off her strange imaginings as resulting from her head injury.

The pain drained her energy, making her sleepy. Her eyes closed momentarily wanting to drift off but her mind said no. She remembered that she had promised Earl she would be free soon. Free to go to him and be loved completely in the way a man and woman should love one another. Free to stay with him forever and never have to come back through the door in the woods again.

The only thing standing in the way of her happiness was her husband, Barry. She almost smiled at the irony. The one person in the whole world whose job was supposed to be to make her happy was the one person who kept her from it. She knew it would be difficult, getting rid of him. He was big, strong, and though not intelligent, he was wily. She would have to be careful, think it through and devise the perfect plan.

As she sat in her chair, she didn't notice that tiny snakes of sunlight had begun to creep over the woods and slither through the window. So totally engrossed in thought, she gave an involuntary shriek when someone knocked on the front door beside her, startling her out of her reverie.

She opened the door to Detective Davis. Ignoring her throbbing head, she forced a smile and keeping her face averted asked, "Do you have news of my son?"

"No, I'm sorry, I don't. Do you mind if I come in?" he asked respectfully.

"Of course not. Please come in," said Lori. "Won't you have a seat?"she asked, pointing toward the sofa. "Would you like some coffee? I was just about to make a pot."

"Yes, coffee would be nice," said the detective.

Lori left briefly and then returned. While in the kitchen, she had checked on Barry who was out cold, then popped a couple of Tylenol before putting on the coffee.

"It'll be just a few minutes," she said as she returned.

"That's fine. I hope you don't mind that I'm here so early. I want to find your son as soon as possible."   "It's not a problem at all," gushed Lori. "You are welcome here any time of the day or night. I just want my son home so we can be a happy family again."

Detective Davis studied her face. He noticed the new bruises and swelling. He had heard that she was a frequent "accident victim" and decided to ask her about the injury. "Did you have an accident again? I see your face is injured."

Lori's hand went to the swollen spot on her left cheek. "Yes, I'm so clumsy. I fell down a couple of the steps going down into the cellar."

"I'm sorry to hear that," said the detective, watching her expression closely. "And so soon after your other accident."

"Yes, I'm afraid the pain medication I sometimes have to take makes me a little unsteady on my feet. I should have been more careful," said Lori, off-handedly. And then, wanting to change the subject, she asked, "So, what can I do for you, detective?"

His eyes narrowed. She seemed so innocent and open. Yet, how could a woman so obviously battered as she behave as if everything were perfectly normal. "I see your car is in the driveway. Didn't your husband go to work yet? I assumed as a farm hand he would be in the barn milking cows by now."

"He's asleep still. BJ's disappearance has been very hard on both of us," said Lori. "I don't want to disturb him. I think he's made some sort of arrangement with Mr. Snyder to take some time off."

"Yes, I suppose he would," said the detective.

He seemed about to ask another question when Lori jumped up and said, "The coffee should be done by now. I'll be right back," and then swiftly left the room.

A few minutes later, she returned with a big metal tray bearing two cups of coffee and an antique sugar bowl and creamer and set it on the coffee table. Detective Davis picked his cup up and took a sip, then nodded his approval. Lori added a spoon of sugar and stirred in some creamer before putting her cup to her lips.

She loved coffee early in the morning. She had started drinking it when she was young, twelve, maybe. She had always been an early riser, like her mother, and had enjoyed their time alone together, just the two of them, when the house was quiet and peaceful while the men still slept. They formed a quiet bond that coffee seemed to be a big part of and anytime she had a cup at this time of day, she was transported back to a happier time.

Her eyes were unfocussed and she was smiling. The detective sat back, watching her face and wondered what was going on in that pretty head of hers. She is the perfect example of still waters running deep, he thought.

Her cup tipped slightly and a spot of coffee dripped on her leg. It brought Lori back to the present and she cried, "I'm sorry. I was thinking about my son and imagined he was sitting here having a cup of hot chocolate with me."

"Mrs. Miller," said Detective Davis gently, "I know this is difficult for you, but I need to ask you a few questions. I want to get to know your son a little better. Maybe you can help me find a clue as to his whereabouts."

"Of course," said Lori, wiping away an imaginary tear, "whatever you need to find my boy." Then she put her head down and her hands covered her face.

He gave her a moment before going on, "Mrs. Miller, tell me about BJ. What are the things he likes to do."

Lori lifted her head. He noticed that her face was dry. There was no sign that any tears had fallen. Her gaze went towards the window. "BJ likes normal boy things. Hunting, fishing, riding his dirt bike. He's a regular outdoorsman," Lori said proudly, and then added softly, "just like his father."

The scratching of his pencil on a page in his notepad brought Lori back into the room with him. She wondered if he was suspicious of her and she knew that in order to convince him that they were a happy family she could have no more 'accidents.' She decided to show him just how unsteady she could be. She announced, "I'll go get us some more coffee," then stood up, swayed and nearly fell to the floor. Detective

Davis swiftly leaned forward from the sofa and caught her in his arms before her head hit the coffee table.

Lori's hands clawed into his sleeves as she held on to steady herself, her eyes clenched shut. They stood up together and he kept his hands on either side of her tiny waist while he waited for her to open her eyes again. When they did finally open, his gray eyes looked into her clear, green eyes. He saw no guilt, no deceit. Only innocence and something else, something beguiling and seductive.

What he didn't realize was as that same moment, she saw a rolling storm forming in his gray eyes. She had been drawn deeply into them, mistaking them for her beloved Earl's.

Bill Davis was a good man. He believed honor to be one of the most important qualities a man could possess. And so, when he realized he was starting to feel something inappropriate toward this married woman, he knew he had to put a stop to it right away. Besides, it would affect his investigation and he had to remain unbiased.

"Mrs. Miller, are you alright?" he asked tenderly.

Mrs. Miller? Earl has never called me that before, thought Lori. This drew her back to herself again and realizing where she was and who she was with, she gave an embarrassed laugh, "Oh dear. Thank you for saving me from another fall, Detective. Yes, I think I'm ok, now." She loosened her hold on his sleeves and dropped her arms to her sides. Detective Davis, realizing he must let go of her waist, pulled his hands back toward himself and, not knowing what to do with them next, he folded his arms over his chest. Realizing how unfriendly that must look, he dropped his arms and then slid his hands into his front pants pockets where he jingled his car keys briefly before forcing his hands to remain still.

Lori was too distracted with her own thoughts to notice how uncomfortable the detective had suddenly become. She left the room absently and then returned a moment later with the half-full coffee pot. "Another cup?" she asked sweetly.

Detective Davis considered it for just a second before deciding that staying any longer would be a mistake. "No, but thank you, Mrs. Miller. I should get back out there and continue my investigation," he said, almost nervously.

Lori set the pot down and walked with him to the door. She held it open for him while he averted his eyes so as not to look her in the face as he said goodbye and left. She closed the door gently behind him, then leaned against it and smiled with satisfaction. She felt certain she had convinced the good detective that her injuries were caused by her own unsteadiness.

When she heard the detective's car tires on the dirt road, she turned her attention toward her next task - how to get rid of her husband. A thought suddenly entered her head. She sat on the sofa and poured herself another cup of coffee, added the cream and sugar, and then continued with this new thought.

It was late afternoon when Barry came to, still hunched over the kitchen table. He awoke to see a glass in front of him with a big, full bottle of whiskey beside it. Now that's how a woman ought to treat her husband, he thought to himself. He got up to relieve himself off the back porch, too drunk and lazy to go upstairs to use the bathroom. Then he sat back down in the same seat and broke the seal to the bottle.

Lori kept replacing the bottles; every time she noticed they were empty, a fresh one took its place. She had laid a ham sandwich on the table in front of her husband, but he ignored it leaving it to dry out. When it began to draw flies, Lori tossed it in the trash and didn't replace the sandwich. Once in a while

Barry would raise his glass and toast his missing son, but mostly he just drank in silence until he passed out again and his head landed on the table with a thud.

After three days of this, Lori decided it was time to put her plan into action. She sat at the table and waited for him to wake up. When Barry attempted to get up to head to the back porch to pee off the edge, Lori jumped up and helped him up out of his chair. "Let me help you, darling," she said sweetly. Then, instead of leading him to the back door, she took him to the cellar door. Barry was too wasted to notice the difference and stepped through the door. The porch is one step down from the kitchen and so, Barry expecting to take one step down and then walk across the flat porch, was caught totally unaware. He stepped onto the top step, then tumbled down the whole flight of wooden stairs and landed in a heap at the bottom on the dirt floor, pissing himself the whole way down.

Lori waited at the top of the stairs and listened. It was completely quiet for a moment, and then… she heard a rumbling sound. Barry was snoring! She flipped on the light switch and ran down the stairs. She found her husband, unconscious. Having planned for the possibility of him surviving the fall, she tugged on his arms and legs until he was flat on the floor. Then she pulled him by his feet, struggling to drag him until he was behind the furnace. There, she tied his hands together behind his back, then his feet were tied together and then drawn up behind him and tied to his hands, and then lastly, she gagged him.

She walked back into the main part of the cellar and saw that she had left a trail in the dirt where she had dragged his body. She had prepared for this scenario earlier and had brought an old broom down and left it near the furnace. She swept the dirt smooth starting from where Barry lay in a ball and travelled backwards to the bottom of the stairs. Then she put on a pair of her husband's big shoes and walked a few times across the floor, leaving his boot prints behind.

She stood back and admired her handiwork. The cellar looked perfectly normal, like she had never been there. She leaned the broom against the wall under the stairs, then standing beside the bottom step, she lifted her feet out of the big boots, one at a time and leaving the clodhoppers on the cellar floor, she stood on the bottom step.

She listened for any sound to come from behind the furnace and satisfied she heard none, she went back up the cellar stairs.

When she got to the top, she heard a banging on the front door. She quietly closed the cellar door and ran to see who was making all this commotion.

She found old man Snyder, her husband's boss, standing on the front stoop. She smiled at him pleasantly and said, "Good morning, Mr. Snyder."

"Good morning, Lori," said the older gentleman, gruffly. "Where's your husband?"

"He's still in bed, Mr. Snyder. He's so torn up about BJ, he lays in bed all day" said Lori, feigning sympathy.

"I need that lazy bastard to come back to work, pardon my French," growled the old man. "You know I can't work the farm all by musself. I'm too old. You tell your husband if he's not at work first thing tomorrow morning that he's fired and he better pack up and get you both out of this house tomorrow afternoon!"

"Yes, Mr. Snyder. Don't you worry," said Lori. "You won't have to work the farm by yourself after today."

"Good," said old man Snyder. "Sorry to have to be rough, but your good-fer-nuthin' husband is taking advantage of my charitable way." His tone softened, "You have a nice day, Lori," he called out as he stepped off the front steps onto the path in the grass that led to the driveway.

I knew this day would come sooner or later, Lori thought to herself. It just came a little sooner than I expected. She had already planned for it and decided she had better get some rest now, while she could. She would be busy later tonight.

Before lying down, she went into the kitchen and stacked her pots, one atop the other against the cellar door. She didn't expect Barry to be able to make it that far, but she wanted to be safe, just in case.

Then she pulled the afghan from the back of the sofa, lay down, covered up and fell immediately into a dreamless slumber.

A few hours later, she woke up, fully rested and feeling stronger than she had in a long time. She saw that it was starting to get dark outside and knew she would have to get moving. But first, she went into the kitchen and picked up her pots and put them away. Then she made a thick ham sandwich with lettuce, tomatoes, pickles, and cheese, just the way Barry liked it. She filled a tall glass with ice cold tap water, put both on the big metal tray and took them to the cellar door.

She was 3/4 of the way down the stairs when her head cleared the floor upstairs. She could see Barry had slithered out a little from behind the furnace. He was looking at her and grunting loudly as if begging for help.

She sat on the step where she had stopped and set the tray on her lap. She held the sandwich up in the air and said, "Look at this scrumptious ham sandwich, Barry. I made it just the way to you like." With that, she took a huge bite, and moaned in pleasure as she chewed.

Barry grunted louder and wriggled on the floor. The smell of his excrement starting to waft in Lori's direction making her lose her appetite. "You look hungry, darling. Here, have a bite," she said as she threw the remainder of the sandwich at her husband, hitting him square in the face and covering it in mustard, mayonnaise and lettuce and pickles.

His grunts became louder and his wriggling more frantic. He began to cough and then choke on the gag in his mouth. Lori watched it all, enthralled with how weak and disgusting this loathsome man had become.

"Are you quite finished with your temper tantrum?" Lori shouted at him over the ruckus he was making.

Barry's choking began to settle and he quit thrashing about. Lori held the cup of water in the air, then said, "To our son, BJ, wherever he may be resting. I hope he finds more peace than you will," she sneered. Then added in a sweet voice, "Oh my goodness, where are my manners. You look thirsty too. Here," and then she flung the contents of her cup toward Barry, hitting him in the face and shirt.

With this, he began to groan shrilly in an attempt to scream through the gag. Lori stepped into his boots, and still carrying the metal tray, she walked over to him, held the tray high and then brought it down on his head with a loud "GONG!"

Barry instantly became silent and stopped moving. Lori bent down to touch his throat to check for a pulse and began to dry heave over the smell of him. "You're disgusting, Barry. You really should take better care of yourself," she said as she brought the tray down onto his head one more time, for good measure.

She leaned the tray against the furnace, then grabbed ahold of the rope holding his ankles together and dragged him back behind the furnace, not caring that his wet face was being rubbed across the dirt floor, caking it with mud.

Barry hadn't eaten for at least four days and had drunk nothing but whiskey for the first three. Lori knew he had to be wearing down pretty quickly, but she wasn't quite finished with him yet. She stepped to the furnace, picked up the tray then spun around and gave his head another thwack before going to the stairs.

When she got back upstairs, she saw that it was fully dark outside. She knew that old man Snyder was probably in bed already. Farmers have to be up by around 4 am to start their milking on time. The cows don't like it when they're late and can develop mastitis - painful for the cow and a disaster for a dairyman.

She put the tray away in the kitchen, piled some pots in front of the cellar door, then ran up to the top floor for a moment, returning in black jeans and a black sweat shirt. She pulled on some black leather gloves, then reached in the junk drawer in the kitchen and found an old flashlight. She checked it, and it still worked, but was quite dim. She silently nodded her head - just what she wanted. She picked up a lighter and gave it a couple of flicks before it lit.

She went out the back door and trotted to the shed. She disappeared for a bit and then came out with a tool belt hung around her hips.

Avoiding the dirt road, she walked through the pasture between their house and old man Snyder's farm, careful to keep random apple trees that grew there between her and the farmhouse.

When she reached her neighbor's yard, she peeked through one of the darkened windows. She could see the kitchen and part of the dining room. They were deserted. She crept toward the front of the house and popped up to peer through the large picture window there, overlooking the side yard. Inside she saw a dark, unoccupied living room and the stairway leading to the second floor.

She ran toward the road and leaned against one of the sugar maple trees that lined the edge of his front yard. She saw no lights coming from the upstairs windows either. It was a chilly night and so they were all closed.

Satisfied, she ran back toward the house on the side facing the barn. She froze in her tracks when a large overhead light attached to the corner of the barn came on, flooding the whole distance between the house and barn with light. She waited two minutes, maybe three, but heard nothing. Must have been a motion sensing light, she thought to herself. I'll have to do this side last.

She sprinted to the front door and listened again. Then she reached into the tool belt and pulled out a screwdriver and a long screw. She slowly opened the rickety storm door. Inside it was an old, wooden door. It opened in, so Lori held the long screw at an angle near the door handle and using the screwdriver, she drove it through the door and into the door frame.

She carefully let the storm door close, then went to the kitchen window, ignoring the picture window as it didn't open. She placed a screw at the base of the window and then sent it through the wooden frame into the window sill. She did the same to the back door and then in the bright light on the barn, the two windows on the barn side of the house. Fortunately for Lori, in the north country, houses don't have a lot of windows as they let in too much cold in the winter.

She crept along the house to the back corner, then sprinted to the back side of the barn. She watched the upstairs windows briefly, then turned toward the barn. She knew the old man locked it at night but she also knew he didn't lock the big upper door to the hay mow. He had strips of wood built into the side of the barn like a permanent ladder that led to the door where they store bales of hay. Lori climbed up and when she got to the door, she turned the little piece of wood held by a screw that held the door closed. Then she pulled it open, just enough to slip inside. She brought the flashlight out of the tool bag, flipped it on and shone it around. It was fall so the mow was full from the recent haying. She just had to push a bale against the door; it slipped though the opening and fell to the ground below with a thud.

Lori pushed the door open just slightly and waited, listening. Nothing. Then she slid through and got her foothold on the ladder, and when she had gone down a couple of steps, she turned the piece of wood on the screw to hold the door closed.

When she got to the ground, she grabbed ahold of the twine that held the bale of hay together and lifted with all her might. It was very heavy and bulky, making it hard for her to carry it across the barnyard to the back of the house, away from the motion sensing light. When she got there, she listened again. Silence. She was glad the old man didn't like dogs as many farmers kept them around for security against thieves. But Mr. Snyder was deathly afraid of dogs.

Satisfied that she was still undetected, Lori yanked on one piece of twine until she pulled it off the bale. That side fanned out like a peacock tail. She tugged on the other piece of twine and it slid off easier than the first. The bale fell apart into square sections about four to six inches thick. Lori grabbed as many as she could hold between her hands and carried them to the front of the house, shaking them apart and placing wads of hay against the base of the house. She made three trips until she had used the entire bale.

Then she reached into her tool belt and pulled out a crescent wrench, Lori loosened a connection from the huge propane tank that fed the kitchen stove. She ran to the opposite side of the house and pulled out a lighter. It took a couple of flicks for it to light, then she held it to the hay and set it ablaze. It only took a few seconds for the flame to travel all along the circle of hay. When it got in the vicinity of the propane tank, there was a giant Whoof! Lori tore off her tool belt and threw it into the burning hay.

The house itself was more than 100 years old. It was a wood frame structure and was sided with wide board planks. Old man Snyder hadn't bothered painting the place since his wife died twenty some years earlier. Winters were harsh on exterior paint in the part of the world, and this old house was looking every bit its age these days. It was nearly completely brown as most of the wood was exposed to the elements, or in this case, to the flames.

Lori ran off through the pasture between their houses, then stopped in the middle to look back. The house was completely engulfed, lighting the sky with its crimson glow. She thought she heard a shrill shriek before the loud explosion of the tank full of propane. After that, all she could hear was the sound of the wood planks crackling as they were being consumed. Worried that firetrucks would be coming soon, Lori turned and ran swiftly back to her house.

Once inside, she took off her clothes and shoes and threw them in the washing machine in the kitchen, noting that the pots were still in place against the cellar door. Then she ran upstairs, took a quick shower and threw on a night gown and slippers. She came back down to the kitchen, put the pots away, took a quick peek down the cellar stairs, and then placed the kettle on the stove for tea.

She went to the living room and looked out the side window towards the old man's house. From where she stood, by the light of the flames, she could tell it was completely gutted. There were no fire trucks there yet. They relied on a volunteer fire department in this area. These were several men and one woman who were probably at home tonight, watching TV and when they heard the siren in town go off, they would jump in their cars and drive to the fire station to suit up and load themselves onto the fire trucks.

Lori stood in the window, mesmerized by the sight next door when she thought she heard a siren. It got louder and louder before she realized it was her teakettle whistling. She pulled herself away to pour a cup and let it steep. She realized she ought to report the fire; it would draw questions if she didn't, and so she called 911. She was surprised to hear that nobody had notified them yet.

Her clothes were in the dryer, and she was on her second cup of tea, sitting in her rocker pulled up to the side window when she saw the red lights coming down the road. The volunteer fire department finally arrived. By then, the sky had grown dim and Lori assumed the house must be nearly completely gone.

She knew there would be questions about Barry's whereabouts in the morning. She had already thought this through and had her story prepared.

Lori, realizing no one would be stopping by this late, placed the pots in front of the cellar door once more and slept on the couch to be within earshot of her makeshift cellar door alarm. She awoke at 4 am, and listened. The house was dead silent. Her mind whirling, she decided she might as well get up.

She went to the cellar door and saw the pots still stacked against the door. She picked them up and put them to the side, then opened the door. She nearly jumped when she saw Barry, still tied in a ball, halfway up the stairs. Lori snarled, "Need some help, darling?" as she ran down the few steps that separated them, and then gave his face a swift kick with her bare heel. This sent him tumbling backwards down the stairs, his head unprotected, slammed against the stone wall when he hit bottom.

Lori ran behind him down the steps and then waited for movement. When she saw none, she stepped into his boots again and walked over to check for a pulse. It took her a moment to find one. The tough bastard was still alive. She turned her face away and retched before taking a deep breath and holding it. She dragged him halfway to the furnace and then stepped away to take another deep breath before dragging him the rest of the way behind the furnace. She looked around the cellar and noticed a shelving unit against a wall. It had been used many years earlier to stack canned food on. It stood empty now. Lori took ahold of the end and dragged it across the dirt floor and set the end against the furnace, making a wall to hold Barry in. The shelving unit had a wooden back so even though it was empty, it still hid whatever was behind it. There were old wooden doors leaning against another wall. She carried those one at a time behind the shelf and laid them on top of her husband's body.

She went under the stairs and grabbed her broom and swept the floor again. The shelf had left a deep gouge in the floor, so Lori kicked at the rut and dragged her foot along it to help level out some of the soil before sweeping it smooth again. She set the broom back under the stairs, stomped around a bit, then went back to the steps to take off the boots and run back up to the kitchen.

Once there, she folded the laundry and ran it upstairs to put it away. She came back down, put on a pot of coffee, turned on the stove, and then went into the butler's pantry where she pulled out a big mixing bowl. She scooped a few cups of flour into it, poured some salt into her hand, the sprinkled this over the flour. She measured some shortening and plopped it into the bowl and then cut it into pea sized bits with a pair of knives. She poured a little cold water over the top and then stirred it all with a big wooden spoon.

She sprinkled the table top with some flour and then pulled half of the dough and formed a neat ball that she pressed onto the floured surface before flattening it with her rolling pin.

She placed it gingerly into a pie pan then cut up some McIntosh apples that had come from the pasture beside her house and tossed them in a big glass bowl with some sugar, cinnamon, a little nutmeg and some flour before piling the mixture into the pie pan, then places dots of butter over the apples. She rolled out the remainder of the pastry dough, then using a sharp knife, she cut a heart shape out of the middle. She placed the rolling pin over the edge, then rolled the flattened dough onto the rolling pin, and then unrolled it over the apples.

When she had finished crimping the edges, she pulled off a piece of aluminum foil, folded it longways into quarters and then tore it apart before covering the edges of the crust.

She put the pie into the preheated oven and then set the timer on the stove to go off in 40 minutes. Then she went about cleaning the house. When the timer went off, she pulled the foil off the edges and let it bake another 10 minutes before taking it out of the oven and setting it on a wire rack placed on the kitchen counter.

She opened the cellar door and hearing nothing, closed it again and ran upstairs to take another quick shower. She dried her hair with a towel, tipping her head over to brush it upwards and then flipping her head back. This gave it extra body and fullness, making her auburn hair look thick, like a glorious mane.

She pulled on a pair of faded blue jeans with a tear on one knee, and slipped a white sweater over her head. It was a little loose on her thin frame, and made her look waif like. She applied a hint of mascara to emphasize her longish lashes and then some of the pale pink sample lipstick that she still had stashed away.

When she had finished, she looked at herself in the mirror. Her cheeks were already flushed and required no pinching. She brushed her hair smooth again, arranged her sweater, then, satisfied, trotted down the stairs.

She had just poured herself a cup of coffee when there was a knock at the front door. She opened it to find Detective Davis standing on the front stoop. "Detective!" said Lori in a welcoming tone. "Please, come in," opening the door wide for him.

He walked in and looked around quickly before asking, "Mrs. Miller. Is your husband here this morning?"

Lori put her head down as if ashamed and said, "No. I haven't seen him since last night after old man Snyder left here." Then she continued, "Can I get you some coffee? I have a fresh baked apple pie in the kitchen." Then not waiting for an answer, she left him for a few minutes, returning with her large metal tray laden with two cups of coffee and two slices of pie.

She set the large tray on the coffee table and then placed a cup, dessert plate and fork in front of the detective before adding sugar and creamer to her cup of coffee.

The smell of cinnamon, nutmeg and apples was too tempting for the bachelor to turn down. He picked up his plate and fork and dug into the still-warm pastry. He closed his eyes as he chewed, and when he had swallowed, said, "Your pie is far better than what they sell down at the diner in town. Thank you."

Lori smiled and took a small bite of her pie as well. They ate in silence until the detective had cleaned his plate, scraping it with his fork to get every bit of the sweet goo.

Detective Davis looked at Lori, this time not studying her but just sat back and admired her. There was an air of confidence about her that he found very attractive. He had heard that she was a mouse, but to him she appeared more of a lioness. He realized he should break the silence, so he gently asked, "Mrs, Miller, do you know where your husband is?"

"No, Detective. Last night he just told me he had some business to attend to and then he went out the back door."

"The back door? Your car is parked out front. Did he go around the house and take the car?" asked the detective.

"No, that's the funny thing," said Lori. "I heard the shed door slam shut and then he was gone. I haven't seen him since."

Lori's green eyes looked directly into his. She never blinked, or looked away. Bill Davis was being drawn into that clear, cool green and when he realized it, he briefly closed his eyes to break the bond and turned his head away before opening them again.

Before he could think of anything else to say, there was a knock on the door. A deputy stood there holding a plastic bag. "Detective, we found something next door."

Lori spoke up first, anxiously asking, "Is old man Snyder ok? I saw the fire from the window last night and called 911."

Detective Davis said, "No, I'm afraid it looks like he didn't make it. They found what appears to be human remains in the rubble this morning." Lori gasped and put her face in her hands. The detective asked the deputy, "What did you find?"

"There was a leather tool belt with some tools left inside it that were at the edge of the house. They have the initials BM engraved on them," answered the deputy.

"Can they be dusted for prints?" asked the detective.

Lori held her breath until the deputy answered, "No, the investigator says it's too damaged from the fire."

Lori looked at the tools and gasped, "That's Barry's screwdriver! BM - Barry Miller. He always engraves his own tools to keep them from being stolen. And that's his flashlight! He keeps that in the kitchen drawer. What were they doing at old man Snyder's house? Barry's so careful with his tools. He wouldn't just leave them lying around the old man's yard like that."

Detective Davis asked, "Are you sure those belong to your husband, Mrs. Miller? Think carefully before you answer; this is very serious."

Lori hesitated as if she was afraid that what she would say would incriminate her husband, then answered firmly, "Yes, I recognize the engraving. It's the same as the rest of Barry's tools. You can look in the shed at his other tools yourself if you want. Someone must have stolen it and left it there."

"Mrs. Miller, do you think a thief came into your house and stole the flashlight from your kitchen drawer too?" asked Detective Davis gently.

Lori thought a moment before she broke down crying into her hands. She sobbed, "Barry and old man Snyder had words yesterday. The old man told him if he didn't get back to work on his farm, that he was going to fire him and throw us out of this house. Barry was furious, madder than I have ever seen him before! He told the old man he wasn't ready to go back to work yet and told me he'd make sure Mr. Snyder couldn't toss us out of here." She was nearly whispering the last sentence as if saying them aloud was being disloyal to her husband.

Detective Davis thanked the deputy who spun on his heel and left with the plastic bag of evidence. Then he turned to Lori and said, "Mrs. Miller, I have to search the house for Barry. I have probable cause for a search warrant," his last words drifting off.

"That won't be necessary, Detective Davis. You can search the house, the shed, whatever you like."

The detective slipped on a pair of rubber gloves, then headed up the stairs to the second floor. Lori stayed below and heard doors and drawers opening and closing. Then he came back down the stairs, checked behind the curtains and in the kitchen before opening the cellar door. He stuck his head in and caught a whiff of Barry and said, "Whew! What is that awful smell?"

Lori blushed and said, "Barry says there's a dead woodchuck down there. We don't use the basement so he never bothered taking it out to bury it."

The detective said, "I'll just take a quick look." He stepped back, closed the kitchen door, inhaled deeply, then tore the door open and ran down the steps. He took a quick look around, peeked behind the shelves at the pile of doors, then ran back up the steps and closed the cellar door. He exhaled and then inhaled deeply, and announced, still panting, "Nobody could last down there with that smell."

"Mrs. Miller, I am going to call the crime scene investigator over to check the shed, with your permission," said the detective. Wordlessly, Lori nodded her consent. He reached in his shirt pocket and pulled out a card holder. Handing her his business card, he asked, "Mrs. Miller, if your husband shows up, do you think you could call me? I just want to ask him some questions."

Again, Lori only nodded, swallowing as if she had a lump in her throat and blinking back imaginary tears. Detective Davis trotted down the front steps and at the bottom, he stopped, turned and looked up at Lori. She was looking at him with fear in those lovely, upturned green eyes. He waved and turned to head to his car.

Once inside, he got on the radio and called in to dispatch to send the investigator over to the shed. When he hung up the mouthpiece, he put the car in gear and drove to the end of the driveway and turned right, heading back to the old man's house.

On the short drive, his mind wandered back to Lori Miller. She was a real lady, far too good for that bastard she was married to. He caught himself hoping that her husband burnt down the old man's house so he would be locked up for good and she would be free. Free for what? he asked himself, knowing the answer. He shook his head and told himself to quit thinking like that. He needed to remain unbiased. Thinking about the prime suspect's wife like that wasn't good for his investigation and he might overlook another person of interest.

After she closed the door behind him, Lori thought about the detective. He looks a lot like Earl, she mused as she sat back down and finished her pie and coffee.

She carried the tray of dishes into the kitchen and washed them in warm, sudsy water. Looking out the window over the sink, she saw a man wearing surgical gloves and a dark gray jacket with the word "Investigator" in large block letters across the back, enter the shed. A couple minutes later, he reappeared, holding up a plastic bag with the rest of Barry's matching set of screwdrivers in it. A deputy came over and they walked off together. Lori could see they were speaking rapidly and she had a pretty good idea what and who they were talking about.

Lori spent the rest of the day in the house, lying low. She didn't want to do anything to draw attention to herself or this house. In the late afternoon, she turned on the television and flipped through the three channels their antenna picked up and decided to leave it on an old black and white movie, "Psycho," directed by Alfred Hitchcock. When the movie ended, she turned off the TV and said aloud, "That Norman Bates is a nut."

She opened the cellar door and listened. She heard Barry's groans coming from far back in the cellar. She called out to him in a cheerful voice, "Hi, honey! You doing ok down there?" She giggled as she closed the door again before heading out the back door.

It was dusk out and she felt safe from prying eyes. She walked along the edge of the garden to the pile of stones that had been picked out of the freshly tilled soil every spring and tossed to the edge. She sat on the stones and looked into the woods.

A slight breeze picked up and on the wind, she thought she heard Earl's voice calling to her, "Looo-reee! Looo-reee!"

Lori jumped to her feet and called out, "Earl! I'm here!"

The breeze died down again. Lori stood still listening but the only sound she heard was the screech of a barn owl coming from the direction of old man Snyder's place.

Frustrated, Lori said, "I'm tired of waiting," then turned and stomped back toward the house. When she was nearly there, she changed directions and went to the shed. She flung the door open and went inside, then came out with a shovel in her hands.

She marched up the steps, through the kitchen and threw open the cellar door. She heard the wooden doors rattling. "Barry, dear! I brought you a present!" Lori called out to him. Barry's grunting stopped and she could tell he was listening. "Before I give you your present, I want you to know where BJ is. I showed him the old abandoned well in the pasture out back. He climbed down to take a swim and hasn't come out again. Isn't that a silly thing for him to do?"

Barry's groans became high pitched squeals. Lori couldn't tell if he was angry or afraid but she was content with either.

She carried the shovel behind the shelf, flipped the stack of doors one at a time onto their edge to lean against the wall until Barry was exposed. His head tipped back and he was looking up at her, begging with his eyes for mercy. Lori smiled sweetly at her husband, said, "Let me help you, honey. Now, roll over." She put the end of the shovel under her husband's left shoulder and lifted him up, then rocked him a few times until she was able to flip him onto his back, resting on his hands and feet, looking like a strangely made turtle. She reached down and pulled on the nasty gag, until she freed his mouth. Then Barry pushed a sock out with his tongue and began to have a coughing fit. "Shut up! Shut up!" Lori screeched at him.

When he had finished hacking, Lori calmed down. Then she said in a tender voice, "Darling Barry, a most devoted husband, the kindest, gentlest man one could ever hope to meet." Then she tipped her head back and laughed.

Barry rasped, "Wha-what are you going to do to me, sweetheart?"

Lori stopped laughing. "Sweetheart? Sweetheart? Hearing you call me that makes me sicker than the smell of you! How dare you call me sweetheart after the years of torture you've put me through. I wish I could keep you here, alive for years and hurt you the way you've hurt me. But I have places to go and a wonderful, loving man waiting for me, so this fun has to end now, unfortunately. I'm sending you to hell where I've already sent your son!"

Barry's face was twisted in fear. He croaked, "No, Lori, please! NO!"

She lifted the shovel up and brought the edge down on his crotch. Her aim was perfect - she severed his penis and testicles from his body in one chop. Blood instantly saturated the front of his pants. Barry suddenly found his voice and screamed, high pitched, shrill, over and over. He was looking at Lori's face and was shocked to see her smiling as she raised the shovel again and brought it down on his neck, stopping his screams, and nearly severing his head from his body. Air bubbled out of the opening in his neck, and blood shot into the air. Lori raised the shovel again and brought it down on his arm tearing open the sleeve to reveal his muscles, sliced to the bone. How many times she swung the shovel, she never knew, but when she stopped, there was nothing but a pile of shredded clothes and hunks of bloody meat and bones in front of her, along with Barry's head.

She was panting from the exertion and stood leaning on the shovel until she caught her breath. When she was breathing normally again, she lifted the shovel and brought the tip down into the cellar floor. The dirt floor was hard packed and difficult to dig. It took her hours of effort to make a hole deep enough and wide enough to push the bloody mess into with the back of the shovel.

When the pile of Barry was all in the hole and she was about to cover the mess with dirt, she noticed that her jeans and sweater were covered in his blood and feces. Disgusted, she tore off her clothes and threw them on top of the heap, then began to toss shovels full of soil on top of it. When all of the dirt was back in the hole, she brought the shovel down and flattened the area, then flipped the doors back over it all in a disheveled pile.

She carried the shovel up the stairs and rinsed it off in the kitchen sink. Then she lifted each of her filthy feet and washed them in the sink, too. She quickly ran the mop across the kitchen floor and rinsed it out thoroughly before placing it back in the bucket in the butler's pantry.

Using a kitchen towel, she held onto the shovel and carried it back to the shed, hung it back on the hook where it belonged and then, shivering, raced back into the house, all the while still naked.

She looked around the kitchen. Everything appeared normal,. She ran down the cellar steps, slipped her feet back into Barry's big boots for the last time, and swept the floor. She walked around the floor to leave only Barry's boot prints behind, then went to the steps and slipped the boots off her feet. This time, she carried the old broom out of the cellar, through the kitchen, and took it outside. Looking around quickly, she noticed a woodchuck hole under the shed. She stuck the end of the broom in and pushed it until it disappeared. Tiptoeing to try to keep her feet clean, she went back into the house and then she trotted upstairs to the second floor.

She went into the bathroom and ran a steaming bath. Her frozen body ached from all the exertion and as she slid down into the tub, the hot water felt heavenly on her sore muscles. Her nose still stung from the rancid smell of her husband so she slipped her head under the surface and blew water out her nostrils, trying to wash the putrid stench from her memory.

Lathering a washcloth, Lori scrubbed her entire body until every surface was red from her harsh rubbing. She finished her cleansing by concentrating on her feet, which appeared stained brown to her eyes. When she could no longer stand the roughness of the washcloth, she pulled the plug and stayed in the tub as the water gurgled down the drain. Then she turned the water back on and rinsed her body and hair before climbing out.

She towel-dried her hair and applied light make up for the second time today, but this time using the red lipstick that she was sure Earl had admired before. Then she slid the too-large black nightgown she had worn previously over her head and adjusted the ill-fitting front over her breasts.

Her bedroom, formerly referred to as the master bedroom, was at the front of the house. There was one window facing the road and one facing old man Snyder's house. Turning off all the lights upstairs, Lori went from one to the other, watching for any sign of cars and listening for sirens. Hearing and seeing none, she felt safe for the night. Officers wouldn't knock on her door at this hour of the night, returning to search for Barry, she felt sure.

Lori climbed between the sheets. She felt giddy knowing that now that she was free, Earl would make her his and keep her with him forever. She tried to will herself to sleep but her mind was still whirling from the activities of the last 24 hours. Sleep, I command you, she screeched to her brain.

Lori spent the night tossing and turning until near dawn, when she fell asleep from exhaustion. She awoke just past noon to find herself twisted up in bedding. She thought she heard a noise coming from downstairs and sat up quickly to knocking. Tearing off the black gown and tucking it under her pillow, she threw on a pair of jeans and a gray sweater, then flew down the stairs.

She opened the front door to Detective Davis. She smiled and ran her fingers through her hair to try to tame it some. She didn't realize her red lipstick had been smeared around her face in her sleep. "Detective, please come in," she said.

"Are you alone, Mrs. Miller?" asked the detective, hesitantly.

"Yes, of course," said Lori.

"You have some..." and then he pointed at his own lips and waved his finger around.

Lori looked at her reflection in the mirror next to the front door and gasped at what she saw. "Oh my goodness," she exclaimed. She ran to the kitchen, wet a paper towel, added some dish soap, and scrubbed her mouth and lower half of her face, dried it with the kitchen towel, then checked her image in the toaster. Satisfied, she returned to the living room where the detective still stood. "I'm sorry about how I looked. I can only imagine what you must be thinking, but I assure you, I was alone and asleep when I hear your knocking. I had a hard time sleeping last night and for some reason, I thought if I looked pretty, Barry would come home, so I went to bed with lipstick on and then spent the night tossing and turning" Lori said, embarrassed.

"And did he - come home?" asked Detective Davis, a little too harshly.

"No," said Lori sadly. "You're welcome to go upstairs and check for yourself if you like. You'll probably find my lipstick smeared all over my pillow case."

Detective Davis felt sorry to having spoken angrily to this woman. She was a victim, he was sure of that. He shouldn't victimize her again. "No, that won't be necessary," he shrugged. Then continued, "Mrs. Miller, we found evidence that suggests Mr. Snyder's house was set on fire deliberately. With what you told me yesterday, your husband is the prime suspect. Matter of fact, he's our only suspect."

Lori drew in her breath quickly as if she was shocked and turned her back toward the detective to hide her face. She didn't want him to see if she accidentally smiled.

He went on, this time more urgently, "Mrs. Miller, will you continue to cooperate with my investigation?"

"Of course, detective. If Barry killed a man, he needs to be punished to the full extent of the law," she replied emphatically.

She spun around and revealed those enchanting green eyes again. Her head was tipped downward slightly and she was looking up towards him, showing the lower whites of her eyes. She looks like a sad little nymph and it was all Bill Davis could do to keep from pulling her into his arms to comfort her.

"Lori, I mean Mrs. Miller, I want to assign a couple of deputies to keep an eye on your house in case Barry tries to sneak back in. I don't want anything to happen to you," he said.

Lori, realizing that he might have placed the watch yesterday without her knowing it, and they may have seen her streaking around her yard with the shovel and broom, turned white. She stammered, "Y-you didn't put a guard on my house last night, did you?"

"No," he went on apologetically, "I know I should have but with every available deputy at the Snyder house, we had no one to spare to come down here. I'm sorry," he said.

Relief washed over her and she replied, "It's alright, really. He didn't come back last night so it all worked out. I think that's part of why I had a hard time sleeping. I was listening for him."

"Well, you can rest easy tonight. I'll have a man on foot patrolling around the house and a car at the Snyder house with binoculars watching from a distance. Mr. Miller will never know they're there and if he shows up tonight, we'll catch him."

Lori put her hand out to shake the detective's hand, and said humbly, "Thanks." He felt a jolt of electricity from her touch and pulled it back quickly. Lori looked at him strangely and he wasn't sure if she felt it too or if she just thought he acted oddly. Embarrassed, he nodded to her and then opened the front door and left.

Lori paced the room. She had accomplished what Earl had required, but now she couldn't get back through the door. Earl only allowed her to come through if she was victimized. He liked weak and needy Lori, not strong and confident Lori, she thought with a sneer. I've got to think of a way to make her a victim again so she can get us through that door. Barry's not here to do the job; I need to find someone else.

Lori went to the kitchen and opened the refrigerator and then the freezer. It was getting pretty bare. She checked the shelves in the butler's pantry and there wasn't much there, either. Lori hadn't been grocery shopping since BJ went missing. Then Barry had quit working and old man Snyder wasn't kind-hearted enough to keep paying him. And since they lived payday to payday, there was no money left in their checking account to buy more food.

Lori did a quick calculation and realized she had enough food to eat for about three more days. I've got three days to come up with a way to get through that door, she thought. I don't know what I will do after that.

It was afternoon but she hadn't had her morning coffee yet, so she threw on a pot. When it finished brewing, she fixed herself a cup and then took it to the living room where she sat in her rocker, looking out the side window.

She considered becoming victimized by a deputy who would be guarding her house that night, but thought it could be risky.

She didn't want to be accidentally shot. No, I need someone else... Someone who will use his hands.

She didn't know anyone like that personally. She really didn't know many people at all, she realized. She thought of her father but he was getting demented and feeble. No, he couldn't do it.

Then she remembered when she was in high school, her father had warned her to never go down to the bars near the river. He said there were seedy people who hung out down there and men who might hurt her. That was years ago, she wondered if they were still like that down there. Deciding to take a look, she gulped down her coffee, grabbed her purse and keys and ran out to the car.

She turned the key in the ignition and when it finally started, she checked the fuel gauge. She had less than a half tank. That would get her to town and back at least twice. She turned right out of her driveway and drove slowly past the Snyder farm. No one was there now. The house was a small pile of charred rubble, blackened beams barely poking out of the cellar dug into the ground below where the old farmhouse had stood for a hundred. years. She wondered briefly what they had done with

Mr. Snyder's cows, then brushed the thought aside. It doesn't concern me, she thought. I've got my own problems.

She continued down the road and came to the bend where Barry and BJ had staged her accident. She slowed down as she made the curve and stared at the tree that she had driven up and caused the truck to flip. She had thought that accident had killed weak Lori until Barry brought her back when he left her beaten and unconscious on the kitchen floor all night. Funny, I'm still here but those two pricks are gone. Who's the strongest of us all? she taunted the ghosts of her dead husband and son, hoping they could see her.

When Lori got to town, she headed straight for the road running along the river. She passed large, faded Victorian houses that had been split into multiple apartments. She imagined that nearly a hundred years earlier this would have been the nice part of town, where gentlemen drove their phaetons down a cobblestone street and ladies strolled on sidewalks with their lovely day dresses and their feathered hats and lace parasols, hoping to be noticed by those dashing gentlemen. She thought she could almost hear the clip-clop of hooves on stone.

A shadow seemed to hang over the street when she entered the strip lined by taverns, convenience stores with their beer posters in their windows, and liquor shops on both sides. How much alcohol do people in this small town need? she wondered. She noticed bars on all the windows and storm doors. Yes, this still looked the way her father had described it long ago. I think I will find exactly what I need here, she thought.

She didn't have to travel far when the street curved away from the river and headed back toward the "better" part of town. She drove home slowly, trying to conserve her gas. It gave her time to think. Today is Wednesday. I wonder if people go to the bars in the middle of the week. She knew Barry had. He didn't care what day of the week it was. She also realized the type of man she was looking for wouldn't have a Monday through Friday kind of job.

Then she remembered that it was the 29th of the month. She knew that the welfare recipients who made a large part of the population in that part of town got paid on the 1st. Right now they're probably too broke to go out. But the 1st! Now that's the best night, she thought to herself. They'll have just got paid and will be heading to the bars to celebrate. That's three nights away - Saturday night. I have just enough food to make it.

Lori spent the next three days inside her house. She re-read some of her old books, ate sparingly, just in case, and filled up on tea during the day with little sugar and no milk. She reused the tea bags as she remembered her grandmother used to do when she was a little girl.

Her thoughts went to her grandmother, who died shortly after Lori had gotten married. Grandma, as she called her, had taught her how to crochet and to love to read for escape from their boring country life.

Lori had read all of her grandmother's gothic romance novels as a teenager. She realized now that they had skewed her idea of what the perfect man was. Back then she thought they should be strong and macho. Now, she realized the importance of kindness and chivalry in a man. She wondered how many nice boys she had ignored in high school because of those stupid books. Those bodice-rippers as her father had called them. They were the reason she went out with Barry in the first place. Then she smiled when she remembered that she had the kindest, most gentlemanly man waiting for her on the other side of the door in the woods. Soon, Earl, she thought, weak Lori will take me to you. Once you meet me, you'll love me more than her, I'm sure, and then you and I will be together forever.

Saturday, the 1st, took its sweet time to arrive. Lori woke up excitedly that morning, as if it was Christmas morning and she were one of those children who lived in a house where presents were piled up under the tree and had great big bows on them. She had never experienced anything like that herself but she had seen it on TV and was sure there were real people in the world who had Christmas mornings like that.

She slept in the middle of the bed these days, since Barry took his tumble down the cellar stairs. Lori folded her arms behind her head and looked up at the ceiling. There on the white surface, she saw herself opening the door in the woods, and Earl on the other side, thrilled to see her. He took her in his arms and kissed her passionately, then...

No, I can't think of that now, Lori chided herself. I've got to concentrate on tonight. She got out of bed and pulled a pale pink chenille robe over her nightshirt, then went downstairs and put on a pot of coffee. A knock on the front door startled her but she went to the living room and peeked out the window. She could see Detective Davis standing there with his arms wrapped around three brown paper grocery bags.

She opened the door to him and cheerily said, "Good morning, Detective."

"Good morning, Mrs. Miller," he replied. "I hope you don't mind me dropping in like this. May I come inside for a moment?"

"Of course," said Lori, opening the door wide to let him pass.

He walked into the house and then kept going until he was in the kitchen. He set the bags on the counter and she could see fresh produce, bread and cereal poking out the top. " I hope you don't mind, but I wanted to make sure you were, you know…" he said, half-apologetically.

"Oh," said Lori, surprised. She looked at Detective Davis and really saw him for the first time. He's so kind, chivalrous, and handsome - like Earl, she thought. Realizing where her thoughts were taking her, she mentally gave herself a shake and then added with complete sincerity, "You are very thoughtful, Detective. Thank you."

"It's no problem. I'm sorry I didn't think of this sooner. But I've been busy with these three cases," he said, his words drifting off at the end. He had noticed how happy Lori seemed and he didn't want to ruin the mood.

"Really, you are doing far more than I ever expected. I'm quite surprised by your generosity, Detective," said Lori warmly. "Can I get you a cup of coffee?"

"Coffee sounds perfect," he replied, happy to divert the attention from himself.

They sat together in the living room, quietly at first until Lori spoke, "Detective, I know you can't talk about how the investigation is going. But can I say something to you about my thoughts?"

Bill Davis sat up straighter on the couch and said, "Of course, Lori, er, Mrs. Miller."

"I was thinking… I wonder if BJ and Barry planned to rob old man Snyder and if they used BJ's disappearance to throw everyone off their trail."

Detective Davis stared at Lori before saying, "I was wondering something along those lines. Is there a reason why you think that?"

"Well, BJ and Barry were very close. And recently, I heard Barry talking about the stash of cash that old man Snyder supposedly kept in the house. Barry said he knew he kept it in his bedroom because he always went up there to grab cash on Friday to pay Barry for the week. Barry and BJ called Mr. Snyder a tightwad and said he didn't have as good a use for the money as they did. I tried to shush their evil talk and now I wonder if that's why they left me, because they knew I wouldn't be involved in any shady dealings with them."

"Yes... If one of them went inside and knocked the old man out to take the cash, that would explain why he didn't escape the fire," said the detective excitedly.

"That's exactly what I was thinking, too," said Lori, sadly. "I don't want to accuse my husband and son of committing such a heinous crime, but I can't make sense of why both of them are suddenly missing at the same time the old man's house burnt down unless that's what they did."

"Do you have any idea where they could be now?" asked Detective Davis.

Lori looked out the window briefly before replying in a caraway voice, "I imagine they are down in the Adirondacks somewhere, probably living in some New York City man's empty hunting cabin." Then she looked at the detective before going on more animatedly. "They used to talk about that too, how easy it would be to squat in one of those empty shacks. That was their dream to live in the mountains like Grizzly Adams. Of course, this time of year, the hunters will be back. BJ and Barry would have to stay on the move. But if they have Mr. Snyder's cash, they might be able to rent a cabin until the season is over."

Detective William's eyes were big, thinking he finally had the break in these three cases, something that made it all make sense. "Lori," he didn't correct himself this time, "I have to run now. I've got to do some digging into your theory. I'll come back to see you tomorrow, if that's alright with you," he said hopefully.

Lori nodded her agreement and then watched as he jumped up from the sofa and let himself out the front door. Not a bad second prize, if things with Earl don't go as planned, she thought smugly to herself.

She went into the kitchen to put the groceries away. There were packs of meat, milk, potatoes, salad fixings, ranch dressing, a can of coffee, bag of sugar and some creamer. All the essentials. I could eat well for at least another week or more on all of this, she thought. But no, today is the first of the month. It has to be tonight.

She ran upstairs and into her bedroom to her closet. She rummaged through her few clothes hanging there and pulled out the two dresses that she owned. One was made of a spring/summer weight floral pattern fabric, the other was dark burgundy-red, that went well with her auburn hair. She tossed the floral print dress on the floor and held the other up to the front of her. It hung just below her knees. It's too long, she thought, but I can fix that.

She laid it on the bed then returned to the closet and brought out an old Dutch Masters cigar box. Her grandfather used to smoke cigars and her grandmother kept some of the empty boxes for storing small items. Grandma gave a young Lori one of the boxes filled to the top with sewing notions. She still had most of the needles and thread to this day. She dumped the contents on the bed and found a dark thread, close enough to the color of the dress and then picked out a heavy weight needle, strong enough to go through the winter weight fabric.

She flipped the bottom of the dress under and carefully eyeballed eight inches all around. It was a trick she had learned as a kid, helping her father with his home improvement projects. She could see inches and feet without needing to use a tape measure.

She ran her hand across the fold to form a light crease in the fabric, then threaded the needle and began to hem the dress. She used loose stitches so she would finish more quickly. Neatness didn't matter tonight. When she finished, she tied a knot and then bit the thread to cut it.

She stood up and held the dress in front of her again. It came to her high thigh in a shamefully short length. Perfect, she thought.

When she finished, she went downstairs and made herself a nice salad for lunch. She carried the bowl to her rocker and sat looking out the window as she ate. It had been a long time since she had tasted anything so fresh and delicious. Barry was a meat and potatoes kind of guy so Lori seldom was treated to raw vegetables.

She had pulled the chair to the left of the window and peered out at a sharp angle to see the woods out back. She ate her salad slowly, savoring every bite. When she finished, she took the empty bowl and fork to the kitchen, washed her dishes, dried them and put them away. She ran a quick load of laundry, and dusted the furniture and wiped down the bathroom. She wanted to make sure the house was clean and tidy when she left. She didn't want her neighbors thinking that just because they had been poor they had lived like barbarians.

Lori always went to bed early and rose early. She knew she would have a hard time staying up past 9, so around 6, she lay down to try to nap. She drifted in and out of a light, restless sleep, and then at around 8, she decided it was late enough.

She got up and took a long, hot shower, then after drying off, hung her towel up on the bar. She took her time doing her hair and makeup. Tonight she applied the mascara a little thicker than she ever had before and even added some purple eye shadow to her lids to emphasize the pale green of her eyes. The bright red lipstick finished it all off.

She slipped the dress over her head and pulled it down over her bare body. She had decided against wearing a bra or panties tonight. She had a little spray cologne left, so she spritzed some on her hair, down the neck of her dress, and then lifted the front to spray her little patch of hair down there. She was sorry she didn't have some sexy spike healed shoes to wear, but had to settle for a pair of black flats. Weak Lori really did have frumpy taste, she thought. She found a pair of gold hoop earrings that Lori still had from her high school years and slipped them into the holes pierced in her ear lobes. When she was satisfied there was nothing more she could do, she spun once, then picked up her purse and headed down the stairs.

She was about to go out the front door when she paused to think for a moment. Then she went into the kitchen and opened the door under the sink. She pulled out the last bottle of Barry's whiskey. She briefly considered a glass but didn't want to have to wash it, so she twisted open the cap and took a swig.

Weak Lori never drank and as brave as this strong Lori was, she still felt the need for a little more courage. The hard liquor burnt her throat and she nearly choked on it, but she was able to get it to go down. Taking in a gasp of air, Lori put the end of the bottle to her lips and tipped it up. She chugged the last few ounces, then pulled the bottle away. Screwing the cap back on, she put the empty bottle in the trash, then pulled the bag out of the can, tied it, and took it out the back door to place it in the rolling trash container next to the back porch.

She went back inside, rinsed the kitchen trash can and set it back in place without a bag, then thoroughly scrubbed her hands with dish soap and dried them on a kitchen towel. Carefully placing the folded towel over the kitchen faucet to dry, Lori looked the kitchen over to make sure nothing was out of place. Satisfied, she picked up her purse and headed to the front door.

She realized it would be a chilly evening, probably dropping down in the 30's as the night went on. She knew she should put on her coat but she didn't want to wear anything that bulky. So she pulled her white scarf off a hook screwed into the wall to the left of the front door and wrapped it around her neck. She checked her reflection in the window and, satisfied, she went out the door.

She was pretty buzzed from the whiskey and had a little trouble getting the key in the ignition but after scratching a wiggly line around it on the steering column, she finally got it in and gave the ignition switch a twist. Her little car's engine didn't want to turn over in this frigid temperature at first but then eventually realized she wasn't giving in, it gave a couple of groans and then started sputtering before it purred. She turned the heater on high, then threw the gear shift to drive and spun her tires before they grabbed a hold and she took off. At the end of the driveway, she barely touched the brakes before she turned the hard right and fishtailed onto the road.

Concentrating on what was to come tonight, she ignored the unmarked police car at old man Snyder's house driving past it without a glance. She took the sharp bend up ahead a little too fast and nearly lost control; the back of the car sliding dangerously close to the ditch that ran along the left side of the road.

She stopped the car almost sideways in the road, then chided herself to be more careful. She didn't want to draw the wrong attention to herself. A DUI tonight would be disastrous for her plans. She checked her makeup in the rear view mirror, gave the back of her hair a quick fluff, then turning the steering wheel hard to the left, she straightened her car out and headed off toward town again at a slower rate of speed.

When she got to the street that ran along the river, she drove by once to see where the action was. She noticed a crowd at Bucky's and decided her odds were best with more men to choose from. She turned to the right and went around the block, then came back. Driving down the side of the joint, she parked in the back where it was dark and there were still plenty of open spaces. Lori realized most of these guys must have walked here from nearby rentals.

Her courage was starting to wear off so she forced herself out of her car and ran inside before she could change her mind. She looked around. It was dimly lit and there was a smokey haze over the room. A TV sat on a shelf behind the bartender, showing highlights of the Syracuse Orangemen from earlier that day. Lori was reminded that cable was available in town and realized this was one of the reasons Barry came to the bars. He loved the Orangemen as did most of the guys around here and could watch them even when they weren't actually playing.

A sign on the wall said "2 for 1 Genesee." That was the local beer - made in Rochester, New York - it was dirt cheap in this area, compared to other beers. She noticed most of the guys had a can in their hand. She sat on an empty stool and the bartender came right up to her. "What can I get you?" he asked. "Ladies get their first drink on the house," he said.

"I'll take a glass of whiskey, neat," she said.

The bartender nodded his approval and stepped aside to pour her drink. He came back with two glasses and said, "One's on the house. The other is from that guy over there," pointing to a man sitting alone at the other end of the bar.

Lori took a look at the man. He was wearing a thick, camouflage jacket and an orange hunting toque. He noticed she was looking at him so he nodded and lifted his can of Genny in a silent toast. Too nice, I can't waste my time on him, she thought and pushed the glass back toward the bartender, saying, "Tell him thanks but no thanks."

The bartender chuckled, picked up the glass and carried it to the man and set it down. She could see him mouth the word, "Bitch" before he picked up the glass and downed its contents. Lori wondered if she over-estimated the man's character.

Lori looked away and sipping her whiskey, pretended to be interested in the television. She felt someone beside her before she saw him and then felt cold fingers on her bare thigh then they slowly, softly slid upwards. It startled her and made her nearly jump. She brought her hand down quickly to stop it before it got 'there' and then she asked, "Did I invite you?"

She turned and saw a big man in a once-shiny black leather jacket with a black fur trimmed hat on his head of long, greasy dark curls. His face was rough, pock-marked, and his whiskers looked like a few days' growth. He smiled and showed his picket fence of yellow, brown and black teeth and he said, "Not yet, but you will." Then he grabbed her hand and placed it on the huge bulge behind the zipper of his pants. The size of his penis was frightening, but Lori was already aware that tonight was going to be unpleasant.

Disgusted by the sight and smell of him, Lori knew this was the one. She let him buy her a drink as she gulped down what was left in her first glass. He complained to the bartender when he saw the bill for her drink and Lori realized there wouldn't be any more coming. Not wanting to lose her nerve, she put the fresh glass to her lips and tipped back, quickly downing its contents.

He said, "Hey!" and was about to say more when Lori grabbed his hand and stood up. Realizing it was time to leave, the grizzly man paid this bill and nearly tipped the barstool over in his hurry.

He said gruffly, "I don't have a car."

"That's ok, I do," said Lori, then led him to it where it was parked in the darkened back of the parking lot. She unlocked the doors and was about to get behind the wheel when the burly man grabbed her, opened the rear door and pushed her backwards onto the back seat. She saw him unzip his pants and pull his enormous thing out, then he stepped closer and leaning forward dropped down on top of her. She could barely breathe for the pressure of his bulk on top of her. She felt his hand between her legs as he directed his grotesque penis toward the target.

She struggled beneath him and attempted to scream but with so little air in her lungs, she could barely whimper. She tried to kick him, raising her legs in the air and bringing her flat heeled shoes into his groin as hard as she could. This only made him angry, so he backhanded her face, before taking both of her hands in one of his and held them over her head while he entered her. It didn't take him long. He reminded her a lot of Barry in that way. When he was finished, he got up and zipped his pants. She kicked at him again before he pulled her out of the car by her feet and let her bare bottom land in the snow. He gave her a hard kick in the side and swung his arm, bringing his fist hard against the side of her face before he took off on foot, humming something unrecognizable.

Lori got up off the snow as quickly as she could, crying. She looked around wondering where she was and how she got there. She could only see out one eye, the other swollen nearly shut. She hurt all over and felt the burn of damaged flesh and stickiness down below and realized she must have been raped. Appalled, she got in the car, somehow got it started and drove home in a daze.

Once there, she cleaned up with a hot shower and lots of soap. She still had a couple of pain pills left from the surgery after her accident. She took them with a handful of water from the bathroom sink, then crawled between the covers for a good cry.

The pills took effect swiftly after all the alcohol she had ingested that night. She fell asleep or passed out, it was unclear which but once she was out, she found herself at the old wooden door in the woods. She turned the crystal handle and the door opened easily to her. There stood Earl, his arms open wide, waiting for her. Lori rushed into them and tipped her head back to welcome his kiss. As they pulled apart, she saw the questioning look on his face so she nodded. Laughing, Earl swept Lori into his arms and carried her off.

Bill Davis grabbed a hold of the crystal knob, gave it a turn and opened the old wooden door. Inside was a large room with assorted odd pieces of furniture, chairs and couches. People wandered about in bathrobes and slippers. A uniformed guard greeted him and led him to the front desk.

"Hello, detective," said the slender, blonde haired, blue-eyed woman behind the desk.

"Hello, Miss Morris," said Detective Davis. "Any change?"

"No, I'm afraid not," she replied, wistfully. She wished just once that the attractive detective would come to ask how she was doing rather than worrying about that patient.

"I'm going to go check on her," he said over his shoulder as he headed off toward the solarium. He had used the pretense of investigating her husband and son's disappearances as his excuse to see her when she first came here, and continued the charade even now. He entered the glass structure and found Lori sitting alone, as he always did. She was dressed in a hospital gown and robe with soft slippers on her feet. She was smiling as she often was when he saw her.

She said to the empty seat beside her on the couch, "Oh Earl, where shall we go today?" Then after a pause, she said surprisedly, "Paris? Really? I always wanted to go there. How do you know me so well, Earl?"

Bill turned and looked out the window, remembering that awful Sunday when he found Lori. He had knocked on the door and when there was no answer after several minutes, he kicked it in. He checked the downstairs before running up to the second floor to find her unconscious in her bed. He saw her swollen face and when he couldn't rouse her, he ran downstairs to use her phone to call for an ambulance.

After she had been examined at the hospital, the doctor whispered to him that she had been raped. Momentarily sickened, he jumped in his car and drove to the sheriff's office where he questioned the deputy who had been guarding her. The deputy admitted to seeing her get in her car that night and drive off but he and the deputy watching from the car at the Snyder house didn't think anything of it. When she came home a couple hours later, they didn't realize she had been hurt.

It was all Bill Davis could do to keep from punching the deputy right then and there. With his fists clenched at his sides, he stormed out the door. When he got outside, he retched and then threw up in the parking lot. He ran to his car and could barely get inside before he began to sob. He felt as if he let Lori down. The poor soul, he thought. Always a victim.

He checked on her at the hospital that evening and learned they had transferred her to the psych ward. He was told that when she had come to, she seemed to not see anybody but looked through them and spoke only to "Earl." After a couple of weeks, she was transferred to the state mental hospital near the bridge to Canada where she resided even now.

He turned to look at Lori again. How hopeful he had been that something special was forming between them. He had felt so drawn to her; she was so fragile and sweet. As she spoke to Earl, she turned her head. Her eyes raked over Bill's face and then seemed to flicker recognition, just briefly. She stopped talking for a second or two, then she was looking through Bill again and continued chatting with her "friend."

Barry Miller and BJ had never turned up. Detective Davis' investigation was a dead-end. It was as if the earth swallowed the two of them up. Old man Snyder's death had still gone unpunished.

The Snyder property was held by the state waiting for a family member to step forward and claim it. Mr. Snyder had been the only child of an only child and had no family in the area that anyone knew of. There were no records of where his grandfather had come from. The hired hand's house that the Miller family had lived in remained vacant for years and would eventually crumble, collapsing into the cellar, as did so many old abandoned homes in the north country. Lori's secret would stay hidden forever.

Bill wondered how Lori had been raped that night, nearly two years earlier. Where had she gone, and why? The doctors had taken a swab as she lay unconscious in the hospital and a few months later the detective found a DNA match to a creep who had assaulted another woman in town. The bastard had stood trial and was found guilty of raping the other woman, but since Lori was unable to testify that their encounter had been involuntary, the charge for her rape was dismissed. It was a bitter pill for the detective to swallow and he felt that Lori was a victim one more time.

He continued to watch her face, smiling and animatedly talking to the empty seat. How sad, I don't think I've ever seen her look happier, he thought to himself.

He turned and strode out of the room quickly, waving to Miss Morris over his shoulder as he headed toward the door. Her blue eyes, willing him to turn around, never left his back.

The antique wooden door closed behind him and Bill Davis walked up the close, tree-lined path, cutting through the low-lying, misty fog coming inland off the nearby St. Lawrence River. A little chipmunk greeted him as he reached the wrought-iron gate and skittered about, chattering. There weren't as many chipmunks in the woods as there had been when he was a boy, he realized. Bill Davis smiled at the cute little guy, wishing he had something to feed him before pushing the gate open and stepping out into the sunlight.

Printed in the USA
CPSIA information can be obtained
at www.ICGtesting.com
LVHW090740020124
767943LV00007B/96